A Novel

THE
ADVOCATE

Timothy P. Munkeby

The Advocate
Copyright © 2022 by Timothy P. Munkeby

978-1-952976-77-3 paperback
978-1-952976-78-0 ebook
978-1-952976-79-7 hardcover

Library of Congress Number: Pending

Cover Illustration AdobeStock
Cover and Interior Design by Ann Aubitz
Published by Kirk House Publishers

Kirk House Publishers
1250 E 115th Street
Burnsville, MN 55337
612-781-2815
Kirkhousepublishers.com

CHAPTER 1

I assumed she—Wanda, I was told—would be defensive. Why
wouldn't she be? I'd be.

I had decided, being my old insecure self, to ask two impostors to accompany me: Billy, an old friend of mine, and sweet Rose.
I hoped Rose, a more recent but lovely friend from the Bahamas,
would help soften the subterfuge. Both were cool and I figured
would be convincing impostors. I expected them, stupidly I now
realize, to act as a couple in the same arrangement as I was to be
in with Wanda. Billy, up for anything, agreed, but Rose was skeptical. Being desperate, I whined and pleaded and finally convinced
her it was for a good cause and that we could pull it off. Maybe it
would help ease me into this situation…and hopefully, it would
help Wanda be more comfortable…as well as myself. This was to
be an adventure, one that was making this fainthearted Norwegian's pulse race wildly.

It was a Monday. Dusk already, and chilly. The three of us
walked up to the house. It was in north Minneapolis, in not the
best neighborhood, and the house wasn't in the best shape. Most
of the houses were owned by absentee landlords who didn't keep
them up. But because it was a snowless April, you could tell the
yard here had been taken care of, not like a lot of the neighboring

houses. Here there were colorful flowers, I assumed tulips, coming up in front of the house and in a pot sitting on the front stoop. The inside door, showing faded and peeling paint, was shut, but the screen door was hanging open, cock-eyed. In the dim porch light, I could see a damaged hinge. The screen had been pushed in…or kicked out.

As I said, I knew that her name was Wanda. Her baby's name was Marshawn, a boy. No dad around I had been told. Wanda was 22, Marshawn five months. I had to knock three times before she opened the door. I assumed she was hoping I would go away, but she could have been changing a diaper. I had to check myself: No judging! Be positive! Being out of my environment and comfort zone, I had to learn to go with the flow. Be open to whatever.

I knew she was Black, so that didn't surprise me when, finally, the door opened. But, behind high cheekbones, her eyes seemed almost to glow…seriously, there was a glow. And a glare I guess I'd say, which unsettled more than surprised me. She certainly wasn't smiling or welcoming, which I hadn't really expected any-way. The eyes, though, burned right into mine.

She was cradling a bundle. The only thing visible in the bun-dle were two wide-open bulging eyes, also glaring out at me from between pudgy, pitch-black cheeks. My nerves up to this point must have been sedated by the accompaniment of my accomplices, but suddenly, the reality of this woman with her baby standing right there in front of me raised my blood pressure to the point I could hear my tell-tale heart pounding in my chest. I was sure she could hear it. I was feeling embarrassed and suddenly tongue-tied. We just stood there for an awkward moment, facing each other. I can't imagine what my expression might have looked like. Terror, maybe, like at the top of a rollercoaster, with no idea where I was going except into free-fall. My mind was spinning but my tongue wouldn't move.

Reliable Rose came to the rescue. She was several inches taller than me and, over my receding gray hairline, said, "Hello, honey. Can we come in? Just look at those eyes peeking out. Ryan said it's a boy. What's his name?"

Wanda mumbled, "Marshawn," and lost the glare now noticing Rose. Rose had a gentle brown face, dimples, and a shy smile. Everyone lightened up looking at Rose. Wanda's eyes then slid over to Billy. Billy was White, like me, and always smiling. I noticed one of Wanda's eyes slid slower than the other. Her eyebrows burrowed into a slight frown looking at Billy. I attempted to seize some composure.

"Wanda, I'm Ryan," I started. Her eyes flashed back to me— both at the same time this time. "You know, I'm—"

"I knows who you are." She stepped aside, holding her bundle tight to her, and we stepped right smack dab into a living room. There was a well-worn but comfortable-looking couch facing a small flat-screen TV poised on a fake-wood Formica side table. There was an over-stuffed chair, with a colorful throw, also facing the TV. Everything looked well-used but clean. I checked myself. Just because the landlord didn't maintain the exterior, did I assume she wouldn't have the inside clean? No judging, I reminded myself. There was one good-sized rug on the old hardwood floor, and all in all everything looked tidy and homey.

"Wanda," I said, because she wasn't looking at me, but at Rose. Her eyes flashed up at me for a second—she was quite short—then down again as she played with the blanket Marshawn was wrapped in. Marshawn hadn't made a whimper. I smiled at him, but his wide-open eyes just stared back.

"Wanda," I started again, "these two, I nodded to Rose and Billy, are in the same kind of relationship that we're to have."

"Oh yeah?" she said quietly, "and what you mean by that? A relationship? I don't think we gonna have no relationship." I bit my tongue, resisting telling her she used a double negative, meaning we were going to have a relationship…if she expected free childcare. This wasn't starting out as well as I hoped, although I had to admit, I liked her spunk.

Wanda, I had been told, worked a couple part time jobs. Both places had reported she was a good worker, showed up on time, and got along with coworkers. But now she was in a pickle: a baby. I had been told a family member had been taking care of Marshawn, as Wanda had no maternity leave from either job. But that was ending. Wanda had been awarded institutionally provided—I preferred to call it 'complementary'—childcare. Along with childcare came me, whether she wanted it or not. It was a requirement of the program.

I am called an 'advocate.' My mission was to form a relationship with both Wanda and Marshawn, at least until Marshawn was starting school, to help ensure he was read to and ready for school. No getting to school feeling he didn't belong, starting out behind, falling even farther behind, and dropping out of school. Not fair! I couldn't let that happen. I assumed advocating even longer might be good. I could envision myself, like, talking to him about how to handle his first girlfriend. I had five kids and I had loved raising them. Of course, I was getting a little ahead of myself.

According to the advocate program, I couldn't ever be alone with either just Wanda or just Marshawn; I was to collaborate, visiting once a week and accompanying mother and son to the required group meetings with the other children in the daycare group, along with their parents and the other advocates. I had been told Wanda had a car but was to assume I'd drive them since often the people, frequently single women, especially in the Black community I guess, didn't have a reliable car—if they had a car. My biggest worry was that I had no experience with poverty or even low-income families. I was firmly entrenched in the middle class and there were no financial hardships in my family or with any of my friends. I had gone to a private high school and college—not much diversity. Skin color, in and of itself, didn't bother or, I thought, even affect me. I had adopted a child from the Bahamas—Allegra—and her skin was a lovely tan, almost bronzed color. That's how I had come to know Rose, through Allegra. But my lack of knowledge and experience with a culture I was told Wanda was involved in did concern me.

As soon as I saw those eyes peering out at me, I took it as a challenge. I wanted those eyes to be smiling at me. I kicked my shoes off and looked around…no toys in sight, no books. But maybe in his bedroom?

"Great photo there, Wanda. Who's it of?" Rose's gentle voice again came to the rescue, easing the tension and leading us into the room. I took a quick look around. There was only the one picture on the visible walls. It was a large photo the focus of which was an interesting and intimidating-looking tall Black woman, smiling dauntingly, head held high, as if challenging the camera. She was surrounded by three giants—men and Black as well. They were all smiling broadly.

When Wanda didn't answer, Rose continued: "By the way, I'm Rose, this here is Billy. Ryan apparently has no manners today."

"Oh, sorry," I said. I was nervous as hell…but determined. "Can we sit down and visit?" I looked at Billy and he crossed his eyes. He didn't look too comfortable either.

"Sit where ya like," Wanda said. "Ya'll want something ta drink?"

We all looked at each other, no one knowing what to say. "What you got, honey?" Rose asked.

"Soda, I guess," Wanda answered.

"Well, let's you and me get to that kitchen. Can I hold the baby? He looks like a cutie. What'd you say his name was?"

Wanda didn't answer and didn't look like she was giving up her baby to anybody soon. She turned and headed toward a dark doorway.

Rose looked sideways at us, smiled, shrugged, and followed Wanda.

As the light in what must have been the kitchen snapped on, Billy and I looked around, trying to figure out what the seating arrangement might be. I wasn't sure if I should sit on the couch with Wanda and Marshawn. I mean, eventually we were going to have to get along, but I decided I'd let Rose do her magic and sit with Wanda…ease into things.

I couldn't really get a read on Wanda. I understood why she would be reticent. Me being involved could easily be interpreted as an insult, but she was going to need the childcare. Of course, holding two jobs was a huge obstacle to motherhood, especially single motherhood. If my being involved in the capacity of 'advocate' was perceived an insult, it was a problem they were supposed to have rectified in the orientation for new people entering the program. I was told she had been at the meeting where it was explained what I was supposed to do. I had to be involved if she expected to drop Marshawn off every day for childcare. And, of course, I, at least initially, believed strongly in the concept of the program—even more so now. The program *was* relatively new. Early childhood education, although randomly instituted in school districts, was not a new concept, but this program was.

Oddly, I honestly already felt protective of the kid, and all I'd seen were fat cheeks and glaring eyes. I kinda felt like I knew him already. Something about Wanda intrigued me, too. She was proud, I could tell. That should be good.

"You take the chair," Billy said, apparently agreeing with my assessment. "I'll just sit on the floor." He grimaced. "It seems a little tense with Wanda," he whispered.

"Ya think?" I whispered back.

Billy laughed. "I don't think she's gonna like this arrangement. She seems pent up like she's gonna explode sometime soon."

"Yeah, well, you know, she's…" I stopped when Rose and Wanda came back in the room and, to my surprise, Rose was carrying Marshawn. He still hadn't made a peep.

Rose saw the empty couch and headed over to it. Wanda stopped, looked down at Billy, and handed him a glass of what looked like water…I doubted it was gin or vodka. Billy started to stand up, but Wanda stopped him, actually smiled, and said, "Sorry I don't have nothing more comfortable than the floor. You don't appear to have much cushion on that skinny little ass a yours."

Well, I almost fell out of my chair. She then turned toward me and just, very obviously, looked me over, up and down. Not much to look at: no facial hair, little hair left on my head as well. I'm sure I looked boring to her. The smile left, looking at me, but her eyes were expressive. I had no idea, however, what they were expressing. In the living room light, they were no longer glowing, and the glare was not really gone but had at least dimmed a shade. I started to get up out of the chair to get my glass of—I assumed—water.

"Sit yourself down, sir." She said this softly, but the firmness also surprised me.

I sat back down and wondered if she was going to toss the glass of…whatever… in my face or what. She was making no move to hand it to me. Slowly a smile, well, no it wasn't a smile— maybe a glib grin—grew on her face. "Are you afraid of me?" she asked.

Well, I was, I guess. This was her living room, her world, and I was not only encroaching on it but supposed to become part of it. And it was a world I was obviously not familiar with. Yet I found myself smiling for some reason. Maybe it was a nervous smile, but, to my amazement, it felt genuine. Don't know why…I was still nervous as hell.

"Rose says you're a good man. So, I'm gonna believe her. Here." She handed me the glass. "Sorry I don't have any ice." She glanced down at Billy. "Rose says you'd be happy with water, so that's whatcha get."

Both Billy and I stumbled around with "oh yeahs" and "great, yeah." She then disappeared back into the kitchen and returned with two more glasses of water. She handed one to Rose and sat down.

"What you gun do when I haul my boob out and start nursing Marshawn?" She asked this quite matter-of-factly. I almost fell out of my chair again. Frankness foreign to my genes.

"Wanda's wise to our plan. She knows why Billy and I are here," Rose said, a grin now on *her* face. "I couldn't lie…well actually she saw right through me."

I looked at Wanda and grinned myself. I was pleasantly surprised at being busted. "OK, ya got me," I said. "Do you know why I brought Rose and Billy along? Can you understand why?"

Marshawn started fussing. It was the first sound we'd heard out of him. Wanda set her glass down on the floor and took Marshawn from Rose. Rose was a little clumsy handling the baby, although she knew enough to cradle his head. Rose was in her thirties. Although super attractive and charismatic, she seemed to have no plans for marriage…or kids. As Wanda took Marshawn from Rose, she was very adept. She had handled babies before; it was obvious.

When I looked at her face as she smiled down at Marshawn, I realized how young she looked. She could have been fourteen, but I had been told she was twenty-two. "You sure know how to handle a baby," I said, thinking I was being supportive or whatever. But—whoops! The flare I got from Wanda let me know that wasn't how it was being taken. It was like there was white fire in those eyes—seriously.

"Sorry, Wanda," I tried. "I didn't mean that badly. You've obviously had experience handling babies. You're very good with him." Christ, was I coming off as condescending? Patronizing? I really didn't feel that way.

Marshawn started to cry as she cradled him, his tongue out and turning toward her breast.

"Well, here it comes. Whatcha all gonna do?" Wanda asked.

Naturally, she meant the boob was coming out to nurse. OK, this was something I hadn't thought about. I figured there'd be plenty I hadn't thought about. I looked at Billy and was going to suggest we go outside. But even with his jacket still on, he was hugging himself, and I realized it was chilly in the house, as my feet would attest to. It was late April, but in Minnesota the winter often loitered into spring. Going outside where it was colder didn't seem a pleasant plan. I looked at Rose, who was also looking chilled. She kept shifting the glass from hand to hand and finally set it on the floor, hugged herself, and flicked her head toward the kitchen.

"Why don't you look at the faucet in the kitchen?" she said. "It's leaking. See if you can be useful."

Wanda was glaring at me again. I realized she was pretty bundled up herself and Marshawn was swaddled in several blankets. I wondered if the furnace was working properly.

"OK, Billy, let's take a look." I knew crap about plumbing—any kind of mechanical stuff—but Billy was handy.

"Sure," he said and headed for the kitchen.

"Uh, Wanda…" I wasn't sure how to ask her without offending her again, "mind if Billy and I look at the furnace and the rest of the house?"

She looked, slowly over at Rose, one eye trailing again, who was smiling that sweet the-world-is-just-fine smile. "They can check on stuff," Rose suggested. "It's a good idea when Billy's here. Ryan doesn't know much about fixing much of anything."

Wanda almost smiled at this, flashed both eyes back at me in tandem, and they were almost smiling. "I could tell that just lookin' at 'em."

Great, I thought. *I'm making a fantastic first impression.* I started to say something in defense of my manual aptitudes but knew it would sound lame.

"But, there's nothin' wrong with the furnace," she said, defiantly.

Billy and I went into the kitchen. Again, I was pleasantly surprised, but once again checked myself. It was neat and clean, and why should I expect otherwise? There was a table, Formica, but bright yellow with a decorative metal edge. Cool. Art Deco-ish. So was one of the chairs: silver metal frame with Naugahyde yellow seat and back. The other chair was broken. The appliances were obviously old. The refrigerator had a big dent in it, but there were several photos taped on. Several of what must be Marshawn as a newborn and some other of adults. Almost all the adults were giants like in the photo in the living room. I didn't see anything that looked to me like it might be Marshawn's dad, though, unless he was one of the giants. Something told me he wasn't.

Billy went right over to the sink. Being a 'have tool will travel' guy, he took out his multi-tool 'Leatherman' he always carried and tightened the screws over the faucet handles. In the sink were rust spots under each faucet. They must have been dripping for a while.

There was a back hallway off to the side with an outside door one way and another door the other. I tried one, but it was locked. I assumed it led downstairs and was surprised it was locked. So, no checking out the furnace. I figured I'd find the thermostat and see if Wanda just had it set low…saving on heat bills was a good guess.

Billy was looking out the window over the sink. "There's a garage back there," he said. "Let's go check out her car."

Not wanting to act like we were snooping, I yelled into the living room asking if we could check out the backyard and garage.

I waited for a while. No answer. "Wanda…" I said a little louder.

"I hear ya," she cut me off. "The car looks like shit, but my cousin keeps it running good. Ya wanta put together that swing set out there, go at it." And for the first time I heard her laugh. It was unusual…almost a cackle. "Dejon'll never get around to it."

"Dejon your cousin?" I asked, figuring the more I knew about her, the better.

Another cackle, friendly but a bit sarcastic. No answer. Guess I'd have to wait to find out about Dejon.

We headed out into the cold. We couldn't find a light switch for the back, but a streetlight in the alley cast a sullen light. The yard was small, and the garage, although only a one-car affair, took up most of it. There were no trees or bushes, but, again, there were flowers visible along the side of the garage.

The garage door looked like the kind that lifted out at the bottom and then you had to push it up and back on a track. At least it looked like that because it was at an angle—the bottom sticking out and the top leaning in. We walked over to it to check it out. It took both of us to lift the bottom up and push it back.

"Holy cow," Billy said. "You think she does this herself?"

I squinted, closed an eye, and said, "What you think she is? Like five-four, maybe a hundred ten pounds?"

Billy laughed. "Hard to tell the way she was bundled up. But she looked pretty petite. Why doesn't she just leave it open, you suppose?"

We walked into the garage. There was very little room on the sides between the car and the walls. But there was a side door just inside and it had a light switch next to it. The car did indeed look like crap. It had been white at one time. It was an old Toyota Corolla. Like mine, only older. I opened the driver's side door as far as I could—a good-sized dent in it…not like from an accident, the paint wasn't broken. More like from a good kick. Again, the inside was clean. There was a new-fangled baby car seat strapped in in the back. Brand new and well-designed, padded and with all the straps and Velcro. Not a cheap one. She may not heat the house, but somebody spent some dough on that infant car seat.

We walked around the car and saw why she probably had the garage door as closed as she could get it. In front of the car was a spanking new red wagon, an old but well-accoutred stroller, and the parts to an elaborate swing set. On the horizontal two-by-fours between the studs were several Quaker Oil containers, spark plugs, and other car stuff. Hanging on a nail was a decent set of jumper cables.

I smiled to myself and looked at Billy, who was smiling, too. You could tell she took care of her little Marshawn…and somebody was sure taking care of the car. Her? Her cousin? A boyfriend? Marshawn's dad?

Billy walked over and started peeking around and found an oil drain pan and some tools. "She must have a guy around," he said.

"Well, she mentioned a cousin. Somehow, I got the impression it was a woman, though." I thought of the imposing woman in the photo.

Billy popped the hood and we looked at a darn clean engine. Billy pulled out the oil dipstick. "Hmmm…full and clean," he said, eyes raised. "Somebody for sure is taking care of the car."

We heard a baby's scream coming from inside the house. It must have been quite the howl because it was loud even in the garage. We closed the garage up, and Billy checked the door hinge to see why it wouldn't shut all the way. He pointed out the broken panel near the bottom of the heavy door. I said maybe a car had hit it. Billy said maybe, but it looked more like it had been kicked, binding the metal rollers in the metal runners so it wouldn't shut right. Hmmm…a kick in the garage door, a kick in the car door, a dent in the refrigerator, broken chair in the kitchen, screen kicked out with the door broken and hanging crooked. Did Wanda—or someone—have a temper?

We walked back in through the back door, into the kitchen, yelled into the living room asking if the coast was clear. We heard another…not really a scream. You could tell it was a baby's cry—obviously Marshawn—but it was such a deep, throaty voice it was surprising, more like it came from an old man. Rose yelled it was OK to come on in.

Billy and I peeked into the living room and saw Wanda changing Marshawn's diaper on the couch, Rose kneeling, talking softly to Marshawn and gently stroking his head. I was startled. Marshawn had been pretty much swaddled before; now apparent was the wildest growth of hair I had ever seen on a baby. I looked at Billy, whose eyes were wide open. I almost spouted 'holy shit' but bit my tongue. Rose turned toward us and crossed her eyes.

Marshawn quieted when Billy and I walked in. Wanda quickly finished up, looking very adept at pinning the fresh cloth diaper, despite Marshawn's fat little legs flailing. His arms were crossed over his face, but as I stepped nearer, I could see his eyes peeking through, looking at me in a hard stare. The look in his eyes scared me. I didn't like it at all. My entire body shuddered.

As Wanda deftly swaddled Marshawn back up, his eyes never left me. I just wanted to grab him, hug him to me, quiet his eyes…but, of course, I knew I shouldn't. Wanda scooped him up; Rose glanced at me and started to stand. Wanda put her hand on

Rose's shoulder, nodded, and smiled. She turned to Billy and me. "If you'd all leave now, I need to put him down for the night." She looked hard at me and held my eyes for a moment; I felt like a deer frozen in headlights. There was an expression on her face I didn't understand, sort of a...searching look is the best I could come up with. I smiled, but I could feel it was a sad smile—couldn't help it. I didn't want to leave...yet. A lot more needed to be discussed...and discovered.

"Well, let's go boys," Rose said and steered us toward the door. Numbly, I walked to the door, turned, and said stupidly: "Nice meeting you, Wanda." Then: "I have your cell number. I'll call and plan the time to pick you up Thursday for the meeting?"

Wanda didn't answer, looked flatly at me, dropped her eyes, turned, and headed left down a hallway, carrying Marshawn. Rose herded us out the door.

When we got into the car, Billy yelled to get the heat going. We were all chilled. I queried Rose about her take on Wanda, Marshawn, and the whole situation. She didn't answer for a while. Finally she told me that Wanda has told her some things...in confidence. She stopped there. What more could I ask? Rose was a woman of her word. Someone you knew you could trust. Wanda must have figured that out. Rose smiled apologetically at me. Just said: "Be careful."

Be careful! What the hell did that mean?

CHAPTER 2

When I picked Wanda and Marshawn up the next Thursday for our first meeting with the childcare group, Wanda seemed OK; Marshawn still quiet as a mouse. I was a confusing mix of excited anticipation and dire apprehension. Was I up to this? Wanda insisted on us taking her car. It was easier not to have to switch the infant seat, she said. So, no problem. The garage door was already open...don't know how she did it herself... and the car ran like a top. Cool.

After the first evening, both Rose and Billy had asked me more about the advocate program. I had explained the Thursday meetings were with the parents, the kids, and the advocates of the kids that were in the child daycare group.

The organizers seemed to have done a good job of assembling a wildly diverse collection of kids, parents, and advocates. Certainly, the more diverse the group the kids grew up in, and interacted with, the more likely they would grow up tolerant and open-minded to differences in color, culture, religion and so forth. Wouldn't you think? Put them all in a position to grow up getting along right from the start. I mean, that would be totally cool.

God, I hoped this advocate deal worked. It just seemed like such a good idea. I wondered if they—whoever was behind the advocate program—had a long-term plan? The little I'd seen of the director didn't impress me. Someone above her with vision maybe? What could it be? Would be cool if *every* kid before starting school, especially kids lacking a parent or, heaven forbid, without even a caring adult in their lives, had an advocate they could trust to ensure they'd be ready for school. Given a fair shake to succeed. Right? Hell, couldn't we all use an advocate? I felt like I needed an advocate!

I had told them the primary focus of the education of these 'students,' prior to kindergarten and with the involvement of the advocate, was to read to them, to identify learning disabilities, and to specifically deal with 'character' issues such as kindness, empathy, sharing, and the like.

Really, what if kids, babies, accept the differences right from the get-go, and that interaction rids them of whatever happens in their lives that changes that? Racism, it would appear, is a learned behavior. Wouldn't you suppose that if children interact from birth with people different from them, in a positive environment, and interact socially, and see that people of all races are innately compatible, they could learn tolerance and acceptance? Why not? And that open-mindedness would be more likely to last, to continue throughout their lives? Why wouldn't it? Learn 'open-mindedness,' not racism. Segregation of the races is obviously not cool. It reinforces differences, of course, not similarities. That alone causes so many societal problems. Fosters implicit bias—which is an elusive deal, hard to put your finger on—as well as outright systemic prejudice. Bad stuff for everyone…everyone!

When Billy and Rose had asked what the objective of the program was, I had explained I was told too many kids get to kindergarten angry and feeling they don't belong and are already predisposed to fail. They had agreed that was bullshit. Somethin's gotta change that. I told them it's been proven it's cheaper to educate properly, eradicate how we fail our children, than to deal with violence and subsequent incarceration later.

Makes total sense. The stats say something like 80 percent of people in prison are school dropouts. Then there's the human cost to consider. What if the violence and crime that got them in prison meant someone was killed or hurt? It seems pretty darn obvious to me…all kids should be ready for school so they're more likely to stay in school and succeed. I mean, really!?

Billy and Rose had laughed at me, surprised at the usually stoic Norwegian's fervor. Billy had pointed out it was also darn cool that the parents and advocates get to watch this happen with the kids…so it carries over among themselves, as well. Pretty perceptive of Billy, I thought.

It's true, the adults may learn from the kids. And then the kids will get ongoing reinforcement and support from their parent(s), as well as from the advocates, to maintain their acceptance of diversity. So, the parents will learn, or unlearn, as they experience what their children do. I understand it won't be the real world in there with our hopefully ideal little group. There will be outside winds blowing strongly, like in their neighborhoods and especially when they start school. Wouldn't hurt to have an advocate around then, either. But it must start somewhere. The beginning's usually a good place. I remember a saying by Desmond Tutu: "Rather than keep pulling people out of the river, let's find out why they're falling in in the first place." What a great analogy for the advocacy program.

Our group consisted of twelve other preschoolers—as I said, wildly different from each other—ranging in age from Marshawn's five months to five years. The parents themselves were remarkably diverse. We had all, parents and advocates, gotten a list of our cast of characters in the advocate program, including the advocates' backgrounds. It looked like it was going to be interesting. I mean, how cool: all these people, different races, from different countries even? Different colors, of course. Different religions. Different everything. Some parents, I knew, qualified to have the daycare provided pro bono, like Wanda; others appeared to have jobs or careers that would pay at least decent incomes. Some I assumed were well-paid professionals. These folks paid pro rata considering their incomes. All, for one reason or another, were enlisted in the advocate program. Sure seemed cool.

I'll start with Ng. One of my favorite names, ever. It's pronounced pretty much how it looks: abbreviate "ning" as much as possible. Saying her name made me feel like a melodic primate. Gentle but primal. Try it. Ng, a little flighty, was a single mother to her daughter Honn and was Vietnamese. The advocate, Maggie—single, middle-aged—was a court reporter. Appeared very efficient. I mean *very* efficient. An interesting match.

Mack and Patty, parents of Patrick, were obviously of Irish heritage. Both had those great Irish accents and ironic senses of humor. They played off each other well. Looked like they were in love. Their advocate, Lou—a married, semi-retired insurance agent. Looked like he had done alright the way he dressed and carried himself. Another interesting match.

Vanessa, also a single mom, had black hair, fair complexion, green eyes, was Jewish; her daughter, Jen, looked just like her. Their advocate, Paula, a young married draftsperson, appeared to be straight as an arrow. It looked like an appropriate match.

Van—right over from Germany with the proud accent and stature. His fiancé, Marcia, was obviously, especially to me, Scandinavian—blonde, rather hefty, but pretty. Their son was Thor, and they had what looked to be the oldest advocate: Maxwell, a widower like me. A retired attorney. He wore a suit and tie. Impressed me by the seriousness with which he assumed his role.

Andrea, a tall Black woman with a slight drawl and her live-in, Juan, a short, stocky guy from Detroit. The south vs. the north thing would be interesting. Their son was Carl, and their advocate was the only one of color: Dale—a retired professional athlete now coaching youth sports. Just looked like he knew what he was talking about.

A Heinz-57 couple, Joe and May. Dressed like they were well off. No idea what they were doing in this group. A son, Luke, and daughter, Audrey. Their advocate, Angela, was a retired teacher, never had been married. Seemed like a spinster aunt taking care of her niece and nephew.

Azim and Maiz were from somewhere in the Middle East. Maiz wore a hijab. Glad it wasn't a niqab that only shows the eyes. I believe that'd scare the crap out of some…at least this, or any, Norwegian. Their daughter was Rhana, and their advocate was Marty…a skinny butcher. Never knew if he was married or whatever. Interesting to see how that would work.

Ona—my favorite I could tell right off the bat—was a tall, regal Black woman from Nigeria with remarkable dimples. Wore a silk turban, or whatever it's called. She was accompanied occasionally by her boyfriend, Jake, from northern Minnesota. They were maybe the oddest couple—Jake in flannel shirt and jeans; Ona usually in long floral gowns. Her daughter, Remmi, was as striking as her mother. Dan, an artist who looked the part wearing a tam, was their advocate. An odd trifecta of adults.

Deloria was a single, rather hefty Black woman, and her daughter, Lanita, was a younger version of her mother. Both had great laughs and senses of humor—their advocate, Rachel, a well-toned, divorced, humorless physical therapist. Quite the opposites.

Maria—a very short, I mean *very* short, single Hispanic woman—was much older than the rest, maybe a grandmother. Her son (or grandson)—Sergio. And Adelaed—the youngest advocate, an unmarried college student. Cool for her to be an advocate.

Standing out, a huge Native American man, not in the least flabby, and close to seven feet—was Jay 'White Cloud.' His son, Arnie, was very quiet and was going to be large as well, you could tell. Same age as Marshawn but towered over him. The advocate—Martin—was at the most five feet, barely taller than Maria. An unmarried anesthesiologist. Quite the contrast. With the two of them viewed from the back, Martin looked like Jay's child.

And, of course, Wanda and Marshawn—the newest members—were stuck with me. It was, indeed, quite the diverse group. No last names, either. An attempt at privacy, I wonder? There was no mention of careers for the parents, only the advocates. No home addresses, just telephone numbers.

If there was a problem that I could see when looking at the cast of advocates, it was that among the advocates only one was Black and there were no other racial minorities. I had no idea if it would be better for a Black child to have a Black advocate, a White a White, a little girl a female, a boy a male. I couldn't see what difference ethnicities, races, genders should matter. Wasn't the whole idea for everyone to learn to get along? I was so excited to get to know Wanda and Marshawn. It seemed to me that this was a win-win. I was going to be doing a lot of learning myself.

I had no idea if there was a strategy in the selecting of the advocates and matching them up with the children and their parent or parents. There didn't seem to be a method as far as I could see. The program *was* relatively new. The vetting process was quite in-depth, which I was sure would prove to be necessary. I mean absolutely. The role of an advocate required stable, ethical people who had benevolent personalities and intentions. I assumed as the program proved its benefit, as I was sure it would, more and more appropriately dedicated people would apply to become advocates.

What an honor to be chosen to fill such a rewarding and important need. I mean, really…to help ensure children become successful. What could be cooler? Why don't more people volunteer? I mean all these idle boomers watching the golf channel and trimming their already manicured lawns.

The teacher, who I assumed would be an extremely important element in the deal, was named Asia. I was told she was, appropriately, Asian. Her two aids were young Caucasian girls, although one, Roma, was remarkably tanned, maybe Hispanic. The other, Heather, a little blond. Although trained, they both seemed awfully young.

Asia had Wanda and I, being the newest, introduce ourselves and Marshawn. The group had seemed very friendly and receptive. All, except for the shy-appearing older retired lawyer-advocate, were chatting with each other. It was hard to tell who the advocates were and who the parents were, as everyone interacted with everyone. In my experience, many younger children often stuck close to their parents, almost hanging on them when in unfamiliar territory (not mine, fortunately), but you really couldn't tell which child was with which parent or advocate. All the kids seemed comfortable with everyone. Several of the older kids were in the corner playing under the supervision of Heather. I hoped like hell the aids were getting an attractive wage – not likely I supposed -- or, if they were any good, they wouldn't last. It seemed to me establishing sustaining relationships would be important, especially for the father-less—or motherless—kids.

Wanda, though, as well as Marshawn so far, was not, as you're aware, as receptive to me as I had hoped. Marshawn's eyes would rivet on mine, a look almost like a threat…stare right through me it seemed. Wanda would occasionally toss me a wan smile but rarely looked at me directly and had said nothing in the car on the way to the meeting. I didn't force it. Kept quiet. Figured it would work itself out if I didn't say something stupid and blow it.

As the meeting progressed, Wanda talked to everyone who approached her. She had already met Asia and seemed comfortable with her. I did my best to mingle with just about everybody—except, unfortunately, Wanda. Asia was kind of a flirt with the men, I noticed. Wanda held tightly to Marshawn. I wanted so badly to hold him myself, get him mixing it up with the other kids, who would glance at him occasionally. But with my blasted temperate genes, as with Wanda, I didn't force it. Funny, neither did the other kids. Several would smile at him but didn't push it either. All the parents and advocates came up at one time or another to meet Marshawn, but Wanda held on tight to him. He didn't seem to mind and didn't shy away. He looked every one of the adults calmly in the eye. I didn't notice him ever smile, though, even at the kids that came up to say hi. He appeared to be calmly assessing the situation. I liked everybody I met…especially Ona, the tall, striking Nigerian woman. She had that marvelous dimple and a super warm, almost alarming smile.

On the way home, me and Marshawn were in the back, Wanda driving, both ignoring me entirely. I decided not to try to engage Marshawn yet. His car seat was behind the rider's seat, so me sitting behind Wanda was not conducive to any interaction with Wanda, not that it looked like that would be an issue. She did seem happier though, humming something all the way home.

All the advocates had brought books to the meeting that were to be read to the kids. Apparently, after a while, everyone exchanged books to keep them fresh and the stories new for everyone. They ended each meeting with a story. Everyone took turns, I was told.

That first group night when we got back to her place, I told Wanda to keep the books I had brought. I couldn't read the expression in her face; I felt something had angered her. She told me I'd better keep them. Bring them to my next visit on Monday, which was at her place with just Marshawn, Wanda, and myself. She asked me, deadpan but with the hint of a smirk, if Billy and Rose were coming on Monday. I just smiled. I was discovering she had a fun, sarcastic wit. She had looked over her shoulder as she walked into the house carrying Marshawn. The smirk now more apparent, she shook her head slowly and rolled her eyes. Something, I learned, I'd better get used to.

All in all, I thought it went pretty well.

CHAPTER 3

After several months of Monday visits and Thursday meetings, things hadn't changed much. On the Mondays, Wanda always had me read to Marshawn while she held him, his eyes, crouched in these plump cheeks, always on mine, penetrating as usual. I felt like he considered me almost feral and was waiting to see if I might attack. Yet he always listened intently when I read, and near his first birthday, he started to watch the words rather than my eyes. His mouth would move while I read as if forming words. I wondered about this. It seemed young for him to be doing this. Was he bright? Or even autistic? I had asked Wanda if Marshawn talked much at home. She had flashed me that glare and said not to worry, he babbled constantly, saying some actual words already. This surprised me. I didn't know if I should believe her. He had never made a sound when I was around, except for the hoarse cries that first night. When I asked her why he didn't say or even make a sound around me, she, at first, didn't answer, looked down at Marshawn, and played with his lips with her finger. Then she had looked up at me and almost smiled, with something like…I don't know…gentleness in her eyes, really throwing me. Told me, "Give him time. He don't like men much."

What the hell did that mean? And why?

Then she threw me a curve ball—a roundhouse: "He says your name before you come every Monday and Thursday. Calls you 'Rine.'"

My heart leapt. I felt it. Seriously. I so wanted to grab him, hug him to me. But I knew that look in his eye told me "No." Or at least: "Not yet."

As the Mondays and Thursday meetings passed, Wanda had gradually become, if not warm, at least accepting. She didn't talk to me much, which annoyed me, because at the meetings she talked cheerfully to everyone, including the other advocates. And she was funny…I guess. I'd be talking to someone and a group would break out in laughter, and when I'd look, they were laughing at something Wanda had said. What the hell! It wasn't as if I was hilarious, but I had a decent, if subtle, dry sense of humor. But I was still cautious and, I hate to say this, but I wasn't sure she'd 'get' my sense of humor. Whenever I'd say something—maybe subtle, sarcastic—she'd roll her eyes and shake her head. No laughing. Maybe a tiny smile, if I was lucky. She was sarcastic, but rarely said anything actually funny to me. Except she started giving me crap. Like one time when Ona had come to the meeting without her boyfriend, Jake, we had ended up talking quite a bit. And when Ona had walked away, Wanda had snuck up behind me and noticed me watching Ona's sweet behind sidling away; she had knocked me on the shoulder, not terribly gently, and said: "Whatcha lookin' at? You better watchit. Jake could kick yer skinny ass from here to New Orleans."

I had laughed and asked: "Why New Orleans?"

She answered: "Why not? Ain't that far nuff?"

I was so shocked I had no good comeback. Only: "Yeah, that'd do it." She then sat down next to me in Ona's vacated seat, and although she didn't talk to me anymore, I got a feeling of…comradery, I suppose. Marshawn was a little shy with the men, but no one else, except me still a little, and played well with all the other kids. They all seemed to like him. I was feeling pretty good about it all. Confused a little, I guess...but then that was not unusual.

CHAPTER 4

On Marshawn's first birthday, a Saturday, we had gone out for pizza, and I had picked up some candles and cupcakes for a little party when we got home. It had gone well. The visit lasted longer than usual, and the conversation was more warm and friendly, Marshawn even smiling at me slightly a couple times. After we finished the cupcakes, Marshawn had reached over and touched my arm. Said, "Buk." Well, I had bought a new one and had it wrapped. So, I set it on the couch next to Wanda and him. I couldn't believe he had, I assumed, known what was in the package and was able to say "buk." I thought back to my kids. I remembered some talked earlier than others, but one year old seemed pretty early to be saying many words. My grandkids, who of course had all been read to and were in very vocal families, hadn't all been saying much at one. I guess some had when I thought about it. Of course, they had all been taught some sign language for things like "more" and "no more." I thought this was cool. But what I really liked was, if Marshawn was saying words, Wanda must be talking with him a lot.

He looked at the package, then at Wanda. She smiled and said, "Go ahead. Open it." He looked back at me, smiled (once again, my heart leapt), and I picked it up and handed it to him.

He grabbed it and quite aggressively tore it open. He threw the paper on the floor and handed the book to Wanda and said: "Mamma."

Well, I hadn't been this excited in a long time. I had so wanted to hold Marshawn and ask Wanda to read...but I wasn't sure if Marshawn was ready. He certainly hadn't invited me to hold him. And...I was afraid, since Wanda had always wanted me to read, that she didn't read very well.

She smiled at Marshawn and said, "Sure, honey. Why don't you sit in Ryan's lap, and I'll read?"

Marshawn looked up at me, like a final wary assessment, and held his pudgy arms out toward me. Well, my heart did no single leap, but started an Irish jig, like a tap-dancing Celt had crawled inside my chest. I lifted him from Wanda's lap, surprised at how solid and heavy he had become, and deftly, I must admit—I had had five children and they have provided me with a dozen grands—so I knew what I was doing.

He snuggled into me, and Wanda looked at the book. It was one of those alphabet books where each letter refers to an animal. Wanda started reading, and although in her conversational speech she spoke, let's say 'colloquially,' quite often, she pronounced every word precisely. The first was "A for anteater." With the second being "B for bear," Wanda made a little growling sound. Marshawn looked up at her and smiled. So, with the next animal being a 'chicken,' she did a great impression of a rather, I guess I'd say, seriously ill chicken. Marshawn broke out in the giggles. I got to roll my eyes and shake my head at her for a change. When she did a rather perky "woof" for 'D'-dog, of course, I could feel Marshawn's fat little body shaking, an unusually deep 'giggle' pretty much uncontrolled rolling around in his fat little belly.

By the time we got through the book, we were all three laughing like crazy. When I complemented Wanda on her reading, she responded: "Well, I been listening to your boring ass for almost a year, I just thought I'd liven it up." Which cracked me up, and then Marshawn, following suit.

When I asked if her parents had read to her, I knew immediately I shouldn't have. She sombered up, reached for Marshawn, said, "Right."

I thought she was angry, but she turned a little smile, looked at me with not the usual 100-watt glare, but maybe a 60 watt softwhite and said, "And Marshawn wouldn'ta had nobody read to 'im if it weren't for you."

Marshawn started to squirm. Wanda said: "You stayn or leavin?"

Well, I didn't want the evening to end, so I said, oblivious to Marshawn's squirming, "Why don't I finish off the coffee we made and then I'll head out." I had an empty house to go home to, anyway.

When I came back from the kitchen with my cold cup of coffee (no microwave), I realized why Marshawn had been squirming: Wanda had whipped out a breast and was nursing him.

"Oh!" I apologized, looking away, "I can go."

"Sit your ass down," she said. "You want to be part of Marshawn's life, this is probably the most important part for the next couple months."

Oddly, I was completely comfortable sitting on the couch next to them, even though I could tell she was making little attempt to be surreptitious about the nursing, and Marshawn was quite the slurper. Guess I'd finally garnered her trust.

When I finally headed home, I left all the books, including the new one, with Wanda, hoping she'd read to Marshawn on her own. As I walked to my car, I noticed an angry-looking Black guy sitting in a black Lincoln Mark VII with white porcelain rims right in front of the house. It was I guess you'd say, "tricked out." The guy looked pissed. I had never broached the subject of Marshawn's father, or a boyfriend, but this guy was right in front of the house…just sitting there, giving me the evil eye as I walked to my trickless, boring Corolla.

When I came back on the Monday after the little birthday party, I discovered all the books had disappeared—no reason given for the disappearance—as had Marshawn's smile and Wanda's friendly demeanor. I wondered if the guy had anything to do with this. Wanda didn't say. Marshawn's penetrating stare had returned, warning me there'd be no sitting in my lap tonight. Wanda had asked if we could skip the evening. I did not feel at all good about this. It was obvious something bad had happened and I could not see it was anything I had done. I grudgingly agreed to leave and headed over to my daughter and son-in-law's, Abby and Abe's, place. I needed a baby fix, and they had two of them that smiled and hugged. I hadn't known what to do at Wanda's, but I had not been comfortable leaving. Something was definitely wrong.

When Wanda texted Wednesday and said she was sick and not to pick them up for the Thursday meeting, I got really concerned.

I called Rose and asked her if I could buy her a happy hour drink. She was a graphic artist for an ad firm and often worked late, so I didn't know if she'd be available. She was dating a fellow at the firm, but she had told me it was platonic. I had met him, and we hadn't hit it off. I thought him a pretentious ass. He seemed to view me as a threat. I tried to tell myself I should take it as a complement, except he just pissed me off. Rose was only thirty-six and I was fifty-five, and with the age difference I certainly didn't feel like I should be considered a threat. Rose and I had met at an art show for my daughter Allegra's friend, another Bahamian transplant. I had liked Rose right off. And since she was from the

Bahamas, where Lou and I had lived for a while and had adopted Allegra, if you recall, there was an immediate affinity between us. Although she had this soft, I suppose sensual beauty, and I believed I rather loved her, I really didn't think of her "that way" and she didn't act "that way" toward me. Although if she did…nahh. I'm an old fool. Better find somebody more my own age…as if I were looking.

I had called rather than texted. I can't believe how much time people waste trying to communicate and arrange things in texts. Some people don't even return phone calls these days. I really don't get it.

But she had surprised me and answered. "What? You're asking me out on a date?" .

"What? No. A friendly drink."

"Aren't dates 'friendly'?"

She was playing with me. I didn't mind. "I'm too old for a date."

"What? There's an age limit on dating?"

I hate clichés and I felt dumb, but I said it anyway: "I'm old enough to be your dad." When I met her ten years ago she was only twenty-six. With me at forty-five at the time, I had felt like she was only a kid. Not so much now.

"Ok, Dad. That mean you're paying? Dads pay."

"I was planning on paying anyway," I informed her.

"Oh, oh. That infers you want something."

I laughed. "Yes, I do. But it's not you."

"Ooou, ouch." Fortunately still playing.

I don't' know why I had said that. I was embarrassed. It's not like me to flirt, especially that aggressively…and awkwardly. "I want information…and am willing to pay for it."

"Oh, oh. I'm inclined to believe something's come up with Wanda and Marshawn. I thought things were going grandly?"

Many Bahamians were ancestors of the Loyalists who had fled to the islands after the Revolutionary War. So, she spoke with a soft island lilt combined with a bit of proper British English learned at school, I imagined. She had texted me often after the initial meeting asking about Wanda and Marshawn. I have terrible aim texting, repeatedly having to re-punch letters, so any replies were usually simple and brief. But the evening of Marshawn's birthday, I had messaged Rose a long reply on Facebook, on my computer with an actual keyboard, so more ebullient. That day had been the best day I had had in a long time. So, she would assume *grandly*.

We met at JD Hoyt's, an old-time roadhouse in the warehouse district near where she works, known for their pork chops and a little rowdiness in their bar. Of course, she had been correct: I wanted to know if she had talked to Wanda and if she had mentioned any 'men' in her life. And I had been correct: she had spoken to Wanda and what Wanda had told her was in confidence. I tried a ploy: no information, no pork…but to no avail. She still got her chops. I reminded her of what she had told me that first evening: "Be careful."

"Yes. What about it?"

When I told her about the guy in the car, the missing books, and Wanda's sudden change and obvious avoidance of me, and Marshawn's reversion—what appeared to be fear—Rose had leaned back and stared into her cocktail. Then she picked up her phone and sent a text. One came back immediately, and by the look on Rose's face, nothing good had been received.

After Rose took a good swallow of her cocktail and looked around the bar…at the walls, at the ceiling, I finally said: "Are you going to tell me what's going on?"

She suddenly sat up straight, leaned toward me, and said, "There is a man involved. I asked Wanda if I could come over tomorrow night. She said 'yes' but not to bring you. That 'she don't need no advocate.'"

"What?!" I said, sitting up myself and leaning into Rose. "If she doesn't have an advocate, she can't use the childcare program!"

Rose sat back. "Look. She likes you. Trusts you."

"How you know that?" I shot at her.

Rose focused. "We've had some communication since that first night."

"What? Behind my back?"

Rose smiled and shook her head slowly. "You guys can be so obtuse, gormless, oblivious…"

"Gormless? What the hell is that? I never had any gorms to be 'less of?'"

She laughed. "Sorry. That's the Brit in me coming out. Look…there are things a woman needs a woman to talk to. She's not going to talk to you about 'man' problems."

"What's the problem?"

"As I said: she confided in me. To tell you the truth, she's worried about you."

"Worried about *me*?"

"You're a threat to this guy. Can't you see that?"

"What? He thinks I'm going to have sex with Wanda?"

"It's more than that. You're a threat to, to…"

"To what?"

"Jesus, Ryan. Don't be a prat. You're a successful, rich White dude from Linden Hills."

"Rich!? I'm driving a five-year-old Corolla. That guy was in a jacked-up Lincoln Mark VII."

"Don't play stupid. What if that guy wants to be a father figure to Marshawn? You're totally a threat. You're also totally out of your element in that…that culture."

"What difference should that make? I read to Marshawn. I can tell he's a smart kid. He loves being read to. Hell, Wanda reads better than I do. He loved it. Think this guy's gonna read to Marshawn?"

Rose uncharacteristically threw the rest of her drink down and stared hard at me. Reminded me of Marshawn.

"Well?"

She sighed deeply. "Your books are a threat to this dude. Where do you think they went?"

I had already surmised where they had gone. And it pissed me off. "So, we'll just let Marshawn fall behind other kids, probably grow angry if what I saw of this guy is who he is. Let him get to school feeling he doesn't belong because other kids have been read to…are curious, want to learn. All those kids in the day care group, play, get along with each other. Now what might happen? How long might this guy even be in Marshawn's life? Does Wanda love this guy?"

"No, alright!" Rose snapped at me. "She's afraid of him. She's especially afraid he'll hurt you. He has a temper."

The image of the broken chair, the screen door hanging crooked, the dent in the car, the garage door all made sense now. "Then why the hell is she going with him then? What if he hurts Marshawn?"

Rose shook her head. "It's complicated. You have no idea how hard it is to be a single Black woman with a kid in the inner city."

"I don't give a shit how hard it is. If that's the…the culture Marshawn is in danger of growing up in, that's bullshit. I'm not going to let him get messed up. It's not complicated to me. It just ain't going to happen. Marshawn's going to have the same chance a kid in Linden Hills does."

Rose smiled, looked around the room, and then broke into laughter. I guess I had been talking a little loud. All the people around us were whispering and looking at us. I smiled sheepishly and waved an apology mouthing "sorry."

"Well, I'll see what I can do tomorrow when I go over there. Look, I agree with you."

"I'm coming, too."

"Uh, uh. Not a good idea. Wanda doesn't want you there."

"Oh, I think she does. And what if that guy's over there. Don't think he sees you as a threat?"

"What? You going to be my regent, my protector? Beat him up?"

"Well, if he is violent and hits someone, better me than you...or Wanda...or Marshawn. I'll pick you up at seven."

When we pulled up in front of Wanda's, there was a car in the driveway. Unless the angry dude had traded his Mark VII for a classic, totally cherry red Chevy Malibu SS, someone else was visiting. Rose still wasn't real excited about me coming along, so we walked up to the door with me trailing behind.

When we climbed the steps, we both noticed the screen door had new hinges and was hanging straight. Screen fixed. Wanda didn't answer Rose's knock. Instead, a striking—tall, strong, attractive—Black woman with bright, dyed-red hair looked out at us through the screen. It was a mild night and she had on a t-shirt with the sleeves cut off and tight jeans. She looked like someone you would not want to cross. She actually had biceps. On her t-shirt was a graphic of an old Model-A Ford with Deasel, spelled incorrectly I thought, above it. She looked familiar.

"Well, well. What have we here?" she said. "An odd couple. A gorgeous island girl and an old suburban White guy." Rose always dressed a little 'Caribbean,' and with my button-down shirt, clean Levies, and penny loafers, I suppose I looked totally middle-class suburban. I wasn't too pleased with the "old" aspect. I did feel a little older hanging out with Rose, who looked even younger than she was. Although this very interesting woman's words were acerbic, her voice was deep but friendly. "I assume you're Rose and I'm glad *you*—she aimed at me—also showed up. Assuming you're Ryan, I've been wantin' to meet you, although I don't believe Wanda's gunna be too excited." She opened the door and we walked in. Although Rose was slender, she was tall. Almost five eleven. I was five eight and not in the worst shape but felt diminutive as we had to slide past this…formidable I guess I'd say…woman. She was probably six feet and not slender yet not in the least bit overweight. As I just told you: formidable.

The first thing I noticed after I slunk by her was the stack of children's books on the couch. I could see they weren't mine, and there were at least nine or ten.

She noticed me noticing and smiled. "Wanda, get your ass out here!" she yelled over her shoulder. "You got company. Dejon D'jerk's parting gift for Marshawn," she said to me, nodding at the books.

I assumed Dejon D'jerk was the angry guy in the Lincoln responsible for Marshawn's books disappearing, and whatever else. I remembered Wanda saying: "Dejon would never get…something, I couldn't remember—maybe the swing set—fixed." I mustered up the courage to say, "'Parting?'"

Wanda came out of the kitchen preceded by Marshawn, who although a little unsteady, was doing a pretty good job of walking. "Hey, Marshawn. You're walking, big guy!"

He stood there, feet wide, a look in his eye like he was a linebacker waiting for me to try to get past him. I definitely felt if I attempted, he'd tackle me. When I looked at Wanda, she had a black eye, and the left side of her face was swollen. My blood immediately began to boil.

The woman, who I guessed was maybe the cousin we had heard about, noticed me noticing as I glanced at the photo on the wall. "Right. That's me and my little brothers. And correct: 'Parting.' My little brothers are twice as big as me. We convinced D'jerk to trade in his flashy Lincoln for a one-way ticket to Chicago where he's probably gonna get his dumb ass shot. He was persuaded to buy Marshawn some new books before he left.

"C'mere Marsh." She knelt and put her hands out and Marshawn wobbled over to her. She scooped him up and held him close to me. But he turned his head away and buried it in her shoulder. "Marsh," she said firmly. "Look at this gentleman, please."

Marshawn followed her orders and slowly turned. The glaring stare was gone, thank God. I wasn't sure what was in his eyes. "Has this man ever hurt you?"

Marshawn slowly shook his head.

"Has this man been nice to you?"

Marshawn nodded.

"Then give…Ryan, right?"

I nodded.

"Then give Ryan a hug." And she handed him to me. "Be gentle with his behind. It's a little sore."

I darted a questioning look up at her as I took him and hugged him gently to me, my Viking genes aroused. But I got the best hug I'd had in a while as he wrapped his pudgy arms around my neck.

"Not as sore as Dejon's after the spanking he got from my bros, though," she said with a chuckle…well, more of a grunt.

Rose had walked over and given Wanda a hug. "This is my cousin, Lee. The one that fixes my car," Wanda informed us.

"And your door?" Rose said, smiling at Lee.

"Yes. Lee can fix evathin."

Standing there hugging Marshawn, I certainly believed her. "Glad to meet you, Lee," I said, shaking her hand, with a grimace. Those were strong hands. Good hands. I'd trust those hands.

CHAPTER 5

That summer and fall everything was cool. Marshawn—everyone started calling him Marsh, Cousin Lee's dubbing—was talking a lot, and, fortunately, to me as well. He asked questions continually when I read to him. They were mostly one-word questions, but he was definitely a curious kid. I had suspicions he had been gifted a temper, but generally he was mild-mannered. He never fought with any of the kids in the daycare group. When an older kid would take a toy or something from him, he never cried...but, I'd see that hard glare. Like: you can take that from me now, but you'll regret it later. Although the youngest kid in the group, he was built like a brick shit house—and big, more 'wide' than tall, for his age. The other kids left him alone. No bullying anyway, which, of course, was dealt with immediately if it occurred. But even the older boys didn't seem to like his stone-cold stare...inherited at least somewhat from his mother. I wondered what his daddy was like. And, of course, Wanda was still an enigma to me. I was hoping Wanda would open up about her former...as well as Dejon. I wasn't even sure why, but I didn't feel right about prying. I figured she would tell me about them when she wanted. If she wanted.

Wanda seemed to be regaining her trust and getting more and more comfortable with me again. I was happy—it seemed both Marsh and Wanda liked as well as trusted me. Although it still bothered me that Wanda was a stitch at the meetings—always had everyone laughing—but not so much with me. She was, I guess I'd say, irreverent—always saying something that seemed to sort of shock everyone into laughter. It reminded me of the first night and her remark about Billy's skinny little ass and what I'd do when she hauled her boob out to nurse Marsh. Which, when I thought about it, had gotten both Billy and Rose laughing. I suppose my Norwegian genes were surprised at the blunt—but honest—question. I wouldn't admit to being 'shocked,' but…I didn't laugh—then. I think I was too worried, concerned, and, I suppose, uptight about that first evening. When I thought about it, I chuckled to myself. I now know what she meant, and she was right: how was this going to work out? Well—so far so good. Of course, that phrase always reminded me of a joke Steve McQueen told in the movie *Bullet*. I can never tell jokes, but it went something like: A guy had jumped off the roof of a building and on each floor as he passed, they heard him say, "So far, so good."

Marsh's second birthday was interesting.

Rose, being the compassionate person she was, had kept in touch with Wanda, so I, naturally, invited her along. There was absolutely nothing I didn't like about Rose. I almost wished I wasn't physically attracted to her. Maybe a little enticement would be okay, especially since she told me she loved me. Any time I was with her I had to resist the urge to not just kiss her on the cheek, but to plant one smack dab on her lips. I wondered what she'd do. Of course, we'd never find out. She seemed to have dates she'd refer to occasionally, but never anything that seemed serious. She had gotten rid of the self-impressed asshole. I hate being jealous of someone I can't stand. I was happy she got rid of him…for her sake, I kept telling myself. She told me most men are so insecure. That accusation made me wonder. She was generally so positive, amenable, I wondered if she was, you know, leaning in a different direction. I mean she was sweet and gorgeous and attractive, but I never felt she radiated sexual vibes or that kind of attraction. Being Norwegian, having gone to an all-boys' private school, and marrying young, until recently my experiences with women and, of course, diversity—she was definitely not White middle class—had been slim to none. All I could contend with was that I really liked her, we were like 'buds,' and she was easy with me—so, I kept telling myself I should be pleased with no sexual tension interfering with our relationship. So, cool, I guess. Except I wondered how I'd feel or react if Rose ever…oh, never mind—not going to happen. But she did rouse hormones in me I hadn't felt for a while. I mean, come on, I'm not that old, and I am a widower, so available—and still able. So, what the heck? The hormones might be aging, but they weren't dead.

I'm not sure what the hell was going on with me anyway. I was finding Cousin Lee, to my enormous surprise, alluring. What the hell was that about? And that definitely was *not* gonna happen.

Since Billy had met Wanda and Marsh, I thought it would be fun to invite him along as well. Billy was more like all the guys I grew up with: honest, good-natured, straight White guys. He was married with two kids. College educated with a pretty good government job. His wife was self-employed. Worked all the time. He'd be coming along as well.

When I had asked Wanda if it was okay to bring Rose and Billy along, she smiled at me. Told me she might have a guest or two also. I was a little taken aback. Was there a new guy in the picture? I mean, I really felt no reticence about her having a boyfriend, and it had nothing to do with color. I'd have to admit to a bias toward someone with some education…maybe a stable job. I certainly wanted Marshawn to be around people who appreciated learning. But White, Black, red, or yellow—no matter the color or culture—I understood she was simply now twenty-three years old, single, and not a nun. So, I prepared myself. There were going to be men in her life. They just had to be good for Marsh as well as her.

I was not prepared for what happened. Couldn't have been. And if my experience in diversity was limited to the Thursday-night group, it was soon to be expanded beyond my expectations.

Marsh's birthday, his second, was February 24th, and it had been cold as hell. It didn't seem it had gotten above zero all winter. It had been so cold the day before Christmas Eve the three of us had just stayed in, wrapped up in blankets. It turned out Wanda did keep the thermostat low to save on money.

Wanda and Marsh spend Christmas Eve and day with Lee and her family, but I had been really happy Wanda had arranged an early little celebration for the three of us the night before Christmas Eve. I was really touched by her consideration. She knew I spent Christmas Eve with my entire family and Christmas Day with Allegra since she had no extended family. On occasion, Rose would join us, as her family was in the Bahamas..

Wanda hadn't wanted me to buy Marsh anything for that Christmas, but I had found a Fisher-Price Barn with a bunch of little animals. Marsh was impressed. Of course, Marsh and I had made Wanda do her lame barnyard animal impressions as he picked up each animal. We had laughed like crazy. The evening had been fun, poignant, and, I guess I'd say, 'bonding.' At least I felt close to the two of them and Marsh was losing all his skepticism toward me. But I had to admit, I was concerned about the next man in Wanda's life, and the effect he might have on Marsh. I was pretty sure, especially with what may have happened with Marsh's father and what did happen with Dejon, that Wanda would be wiser. She had obviously gained self-confidence. I was confident she would not just settle but be more discerning about her choices. I guessed I'd be finding out soon.

When I called Wanda to see what plans we should make for Marsh's second birthday, where and how many, she just said Billy, Rose, and I should just cross our fingers and show up. She gave me an address on Broadway Avenue in Minneapolis where we would be celebrating. I knew a little about the neighborhood and that the area was a little sketchy. Broadway had a reputation. When I asked whose home, she laughed and said it wasn't a house. Just show up about noon since it was on a Sunday this year. No need to bring anything but my and Billy's skinny asses…and Rose.

Rose and Billy drove over to my Linden Hills Cape Cod, and I drove, having the oldest, least attractive car. Both of them had new, rather fancy vehicles. Rose thought when I had suggested it that I was being paranoid. Billy knew the neighborhood, somewhat near where he had grown up, and thought it wasn't a bad idea. As I said, Broadway had a reputation.

The address led us to an old stucco building converted, apparently, to an auto shop with a half-dozen bay doors and an office entrance with the name "Deseal Bros and Big Sis" above the door. There were nine or ten motorcycles and eleven or twelve cars parked randomly around the building. The cars ranged from brand-new Cadillacs to pile-of-shit clunkers. We could hear music coming from inside.

When we knocked on the office door, a guy—I swear he was eight feet tall and just as wide, opened the door and boomed in the voice of a grizzly bear: "What ya'll knocking for? Come on in and join the party." He had on the same t-shirt Lee had had on—only black with a yellow Model-T and the name 'Deseal' on it. I recalled Lee's had had 'Deseal' on hers, too. I wondered if all Model-Ts had been diesels, and, again, if they were spelling diesel wrong.

"I'm Clyde, one of little Wanda's brothers." Still booming. He stuck out a huge, meaty paw, colorful tattoos running up the largest black arm, actually just the largest arm I'd ever seen. "I'm guessing from what I've heard you're Ryan," Clyde said as he gently shook my hand. And "Oohee, honey, you must be Rose. Wanda weren't kiddin' what a killer you be. Ooee." He gently took Rose's hand in his fingers, bent, and kissed it.

Rose laughed, her dimple working its magic, and said, "Man, you are the most enormous gentleman I've ever had the pleasure of kissing my hand. Glad to meet you, Clyde."

Clyde turned to Billy: "And you my man is who?"

When Billy told him, he said, "The fellow dat fixed Wanda's faucet? Cool, man," and shook his hand. "Ya'll come on in and meet the bros." He snatched up the presents we were carrying, and we followed him.

They had cleaned out one of the bays and it was mostly filled with giants. When Marsh saw me, he plodded over and wrapped his arm around my leg. I was totally frickin' excited and picked him up for a hug. But he had decided he wasn't much of a hugger today, and after a second pushed away and slid to the floor. He pointed to Billy. Did he remember him? And Rose bent down, snatched him up, and said, "How bout a kiss?" To my surprise, he kissed her on the cheek. Also to my surprise, Wanda came up and gave me a little hug. My first.

When I turned to Lee, I stuck my hand out to shake it. She slapped it away, bent down, wrapped me in strong arms, snuggling me comfortably between her rather impressive bosoms. I didn't mind…far from it. She set me free and said, "Thank you Ryan. We're all glad what yur doin' fur Ryan." Tapped me on the cheek in a gentle slap and introduced me to Clyde's three brothers—almost as large as Clyde—Claude and Clay and Albert. With Clyde, Claude, and Clay—all "C's"—I wondered if it because Albert was the most rotund...you know—"Fat Albert." Of course, I didn't say anything. Offending one of these guys could be your final offense. I could see why Dejon D'jerk left town. He was either a fool, had a death wish, or both to dare smack Wanda, much less whatever he did to Marsh. I wondered if Dejon, or even Marsh's father, who also was apparently not around, had anything to do with Wanda's lazy eye. I wondered if Marsh's sore bottom also had something to do with D'jerk. I'm guessing that would have been suicide. Maybe he wasn't in Chicago but Lake Michigan?

Well, the party was a riot. Marsh got a lot of gifts, and he was so excited he was beside himself. I had gotten him a kid's 'tablet.' I guess that's what you'd call it. I figured he'd better get used to buttons—like a lot of the other 'privileged' kids. He was immediately interested—no fear of buttons. I hoped Wanda approved. The Deseals were like a dog I once had. A Great Pyrenees. Fearful looking, but a gentle giant. I hadn't laughed so much in a long time. Billy and, naturally, Rose also had a great time.

I found out later that the Deseal—now I felt foolish thinking they had misspelled diesel—brothers pretty much took care of the minorities' cars on the north side. When I had asked Clyde, sometime later, about it, he had said: "A lot of the poor guys and women on the north side couldn't afford to keep their cars up, so the ones with dough, gleaned from one place or another, basically covered their cost." He had said, "If a Black guy took a car to the dealership, he got screwed, pardon my French. So, they bring them to us. Some pay a little more than the others, but still come out better. They don't complain."

So, a form of social democracy on the poverty-stricken north side. Cool. Way ahead of their time.

CHAPTER 6

That spring, summer, and fall, everything was going well. Marsh'd try to read along with us, with either the books I bought or ones we had traded at group—but would get pretty frustrated. I started to see he did indeed have a temper. But at group he got along fine. He was getting big…the same size as the three and some of the four-year-olds, except for Arnie White-cloud…and, as I've said, was built like a linebacker. A couple of the families moved away, and a couple of the kids started kinder-garten, but they, interestingly, wanted to remain in the group. The parents and advocates had all become close. We had some picnics in the summer, once visited a nursing home, which was a big hit with everyone—the kids, the adults, and the old folks. Oddly, Asia never showed up for these 'events,' and they were arranged mostly by the advocates.

All through the fall into winter, Marsh, although still relatively reserved, was clearly gaining self-assurance. If one of the boys had taken something from one of the girls, Marsh would retrieve it and hand it back. None of the boys would argue with Marsh. I give credit to Dejon and his apparent abuse of Wanda for that—Marsh was going to protect the ladies in his life. I had figured out that glaring stare I had gotten was Marsh warning me not to hurt his mother, and he used the same glare in the group, warning the older boys not to bully the girls. Cool, I thought—at the time.

There was no tension, among the kids, parents, or advocates, due to race, ethnicity, religion, gender, or any of the common prejudices. The program was working remarkably well in that regard. Although one of the aids had, as I had feared, left—they were not paid well enough—fortunately the teacher, Asia, had remained the same. She was single and did a pretty good job organizing the Thursday activities. We had all—parents and advocates—learned how to encourage the kids to treat each other with kindness and respect. Asia and the aids had specific exercises and games where we practiced empathy, compassion, and trust. Cool, definitely.

A couple new families had joined the group: another single Black mother, Latoya, with a little two-year-old girl, cute as a button; and a Russian lesbian couple, Cheryl and Simone, who had adopted a one-year-old girl from their homeland. The diversity was amazing and growing.

Ona, the pretty Nigerian woman, had broken up with her boyfriend. As I believe I've mentioned, she had the most beautiful smile, as did her cute, respectful little three-year-old, Remmi. Ona was especially attentive to Marsh. Although she was a little younger than me…well considerably younger actually…I considered asking her out. But, we had become friends, so I demurred, for now, once again reminding myself I needed to act my age. I started wondering about my hormones. They had been latent for some time but seemed to be coming alive. I was discovering, the more comfortable I was getting outside of my old conventional culture, the more willing I was becoming to throw out conventions and contemplate new adventures. Explore a bit. Screw acting my age!

As I mentioned, I spend Christmas Day with Allegra, since she was single and adopted, and so had no extended family. We would generally go to a movie and out to eat. Christmas Eve involved the entire family. My son, Christopher, the oldest, and his wife, Lizzy, and four kids—Jake, Samara, Jax, and Maci—now hosted Christmas. The rest of the family included my four married daughters: the oldest, McGenty (Mac), married to a great guy we call Hiball, and their three: Hadley, Walt, and Abilene. The youngest are the twins: Abby married to Abe. (We were worried about the union of two people with these cute similar, alliterating names. But in-laws are potluck: you got nothing to say about it and can hardly expect them to change their names.) Their two: Sadie, close to Marsh's age, and Randi, our baby; Edie, the other twin, married to Tad with their two boys—Levi and Berti. Not many traditional names in there. Then there was Allegra, a year older than my twins, whom Lou and I had, as I've said, adopted while living in the Bahamas. Allegra reminded me of Rose, naturally since both are Bahamian. Both had this silky-brown complexion and were demure and soft-spoken. Although when riled, Allegra could wreak havoc on…usually me. Maybe Rose had thorns I just hadn't been exposed to, yet?

Lou and I used to host the Christmas Eve festivities. But after Louise died, my son and daughter-in-law took over. They had created a well-endowed play area in their lower level that kept the kids occupied while the adults enjoyed their Christmas cheers upstairs.

On our way back home after our Thursday meeting in early December, I had asked Wanda if she and Marsh would like to spend some time at Christmas with me and my family that year.

Wanda looked at me for a while, looked straight ahead, then back to me. "So, a White Christmas then?"

That cracked me up. Finally, her wit whetted in my direction. Wanda had been a little more willing lately to share her sense of humor…though usually at my expense.

"Not completely," I answered.

She looked back and forth at me and the road—she still insisted on driving—and repeated, "Not completely? What's that supposed to mean?"

I smiled, "Well, you'll have to accept my invitation to find out."

Marsh, who was usually quiet in his car seat in the back, would get a little frustrated at being strapped in. Yelled: "Any kids dere?"

Wanda looked in the rearview mirror and corrected: "Will there be any other kids there?" enunciating clearly.

"Uncle Deas's don't talk like dat."

"You can talk like 'dat' to all the Uncle Deas's—when you're with them. You don't talk like that at our meetings, do ya?"

"'You!'" he shouted rather vibrantly.

I spun around and looked at Marsh, I'm sure a frown on my face. First, even though I figured he just might have a little temper stored up inside him, the shout *surprised* me really. Second, the tone was definitely cheeky, maybe even insolent. Wanda's eyes, reflecting in the mirror, got that glare that I was well acquainted with.

Looking at Marsh, he didn't have that 'oh shit-what-did-I-do?' look. When he smiled at me, I realized what he was doing. He was correcting his mother because she had corrected him. When I turned to Wanda with a big smile on my face, she flung—both eyes flying—that frightening glare over at me.

When I started to explain what I thought would be vindication for Marsh's rather clever response, she shook her head—nothing new—and cut me off.

She had been staring him down in the mirror, the glare not relenting. I was getting a little concerned. She was a good driver, but she was spending a lot of time in a stare down with her son. I picked up on the little skirmish going on. You know in a stare down the first one to look away loses, right? Well, Marsh couldn't lose, and I think he knew it. No, I know he knew it. They would have their eyes locked, but eventually Wanda'd have to glance at the road. When she would glance back, Marsh was still staring at her. Marsh had won, and they'd start over, again. Several times my foot pushed on the imaginary break, and I was considering taking over the wheel…but put that out of my mind quickly.

It was marvelous watching this kid, who sure seemed smart for a two-year-old…heck, for a 60-year-old, playing mind games with his mother. Then, when Wanda was making a turn, he glanced at me and smiled. That's when I knew for sure. But when Wanda looked back and saw the smile fading on his face, she lost her temper, especially since she had figured out her little fella couldn't lose and she couldn't win. She grabbed the wheel firmly with both hands and said loudly and steely, without looking in the rearview mirror, her teeth grinding: "You listen to me boy, and listen good!" (Funny how different cultures, different levels of education, amount of net worth, they all say the same shit scolding their kids.) "You don't ever talk to me in that tone, again. AND, I *can* correct you. You cannot correct your mother. You hear me young man?" She didn't look at him in the mirror anymore.

He looked at me and smiled. "Can I correct Uncle Rine?" OK, sorry to be sappy, but I had that old heart leap thing again. He had never called me 'uncle' before.

Now she looked in the mirror and started: "Don't change the…" but Marsh had such an inculpable look on his face, I saw her try to hide a smile. She cleared her throat, tried to sound gruff: "No, you cannot correct adults." She looked over at me. "Your 'uncle' Ryan might not seem like an adult most of the time, but, no, you should not correct him, either."

I was going to banter with something like, "Well, what's to correct?" but thought better of it. It would work with my kids or friends, who would just groan and give a stupid comeback. So, I just smiled and shut up like a good Norwegian.

"Nobody be talking like Uncle Deas's dere?"

Wanda now looked in the review mirror, shaking her head at Marsh, not me for a change. "Where?"

"At Uncle Ryan's?" The little shit actually said "Ryan."

Wanda didn't catch it. "No. Nobody's going to talk like that at Ryan's house. Nor would your uncles or aunt, either. And your cousins don't talk like that." I looked over at Wanda.

"Who cousins?" Marsh asked.

She let that one slide. "Uncle Ryan's family—they will talk properly."

"I know."

'Alleluia' I thought to myself. First, I was happy she referred to my grandkids as Marsh's 'cousins.' And, secondly, if he could figure that out now, how to speak when and where, at his age, a huge hurdle will have been mastered. It's been good for Wanda as well to be aware of this. She still usually used her colloquial vernacular not only with her cousins, but with me...mostly to bug me I thought. Although she corrected Marsh regularly, it irritated her that she knew I was annoyed when she spoke too homey...that Marsh would be more likely to use 'street' if she did. At group, though, she enunciated concisely, I had noticed. So did Marsh.

I was getting excited. It sounded as if she might be accepting the Christmas invitation.

"Well?" I said to Wanda.

She took a while, again, to answer. "We'll see." After a pause and with a slight smile: "Thanks fur askin', Rine."

It turned out Wanda's cousins and other family were all going down to Chicago to the Deasels' mom's for Christmas. Wanda felt she couldn't afford to get to Chicago and wouldn't accept 'charity' from her cousins. I knew nothing about where her mother or father were. So, yea, she accepted my invitation, if a little hesitantly, saying: "No snow up here yet, but it looks like I'll be gettin' dat White Christmas, anyhoo."

"Remember, 'not completely,'" I had said, laughing.

"What you talkin', boy?" she said to bug me.

"You'll see," I said, smiling.

As I said, my son and daughter-in-law had turned the lower level of their rather expansive home into an indoor playground. Lizzie had done most of the designing, and more than her fair share of the work. Which was fair, I thought, since Chis had a good enough career that Lizzie could stay home with the kids...not that the kids weren't a full-time job, but they were all in school now and some driving. (I think I better change the subject; I'd probably be getting myself in trouble here if my kids could hear me, thinking I'm talking sexist.) Lizzy was a master with a hammer and a saw...as well as a master photographer. Anyway, it was pretty much a sound-proof padded cell. The main room had two nets at each end which were used for shooting hockey pucks or tennis balls and kicking soccer balls. There were swings for the little ones, a tricking bar, mats on the floor for wrestling, tumbling...whatever. The walls were actually padded...nothing exposed that could be broken, except bones, and, hopefully, the padding minimized that.

A second smaller room had a large screen TV and a variety of technical paraphernalia...all which could be broken. So, no balls, pucks, etc. in there. Like I said: a modern indoor playground. A kid's utopia. Meanwhile the adults would be upstairs chatting, drinking, and hors d'oeuvr-ing, far from the madding crowd below.

Christmas Eve, Wanda let me pick her and Marsh up for a change. She was leery of navigating the winding, wood-lined roads around the lakes in the western suburbs, as opposed to the gridded rectangles of the city. I could tell she was nervous about the evening because she talked non-stop on the drive there. Highly unusual. Usually, I had to almost threaten to pry out of her very peculiar mind what she was thinking. She had become an enigma to me, which I think I've already indicated. She was obviously smart. Could be very sarcastic. At times spoke almost eloquently in metaphors. Other times she would appear to be clueless, cultureless, and I could barely understand her 'casual' dialect—as she called it. Sometimes I felt like she was doing this mischievously, other times almost spitefully. She could be charming and endearing…easy to like and comfortable to be with. She could also, for no apparent reason, get her ire up and the frightening glare would appear, scaring the crap out of me.

Tonight, she rambled randomly but I found myself smiling continuously. I would peek at Marsh in the rearview mirror and smile at him, and now get at least a flicker of a smile in return. He seemed to have become irreversibly, I hoped, comfortable with me and would always hug me now when we saw each other. I wasn't sure if Wanda put him up to this or not…but I didn't care. Nothing, excepting my own family, made me happier. He could talk my ear off sometimes…but, tonight, he was quiet, not that he could get a word in edgewise, but obviously contemplative about what this evening's adventure would entail. I couldn't wait.

When we arrived at Chris and Lizzie's, Marshawn grabbed my hand as we walked up to the door. This had never happened before. Marsh was proud, and his independence would usually not have allowed a handhold.

Wanda walked behind us, like she was masking her arrival. I had told her she needn't buy any Christmas presents since there would be too many people to buy for, but she had one under her arm, nicely wrapped. We had gone out and, despite her resistance, I had bought Marsh some presents which were to be from Santa Claus for Christmas morning, so left at home. Except I had one in my other hand for tonight. She had argued she had bought all he needed, and he would get 'spoilt.' I had also brought along a present for Wanda, which was in my pocket.

When we opened the door, we were fell upon by a hoard of loud, riotous children. With a few brief greetings of "hi Grandpa," all initially ignored Wanda. Samara—the oldest of the girls—swooped up Marshawn, all my grands shouting "Mar-shawn, Mar-shawn" and swept him away in a crush of pubescence that disappeared down into the den of merriment and hijinks, Sadie trailing behind and Maci carrying baby Randi. Jake, Jax, and Walt -- the boys -- headed for my car to collect my gifts for the grandkids.

Wanda stood there, mouth agape, both eyes trailing her little son's wake as he was shipped away. "Don't worry," I told her, "they'll bring him back when it's time to open presents."

She looked at me. I couldn't tell what she was thinking. She probably didn't know, either. She looked back and forth from the doorway and me a couple times and finally said: "Will they bring him back alive?"

This cracked me up and I grabbed her hand—the first time I had ever really initiated a touch—and led her into the kitchen, the room where everyone in my family has always hung out. A family rule: you had to have a big kitchen.

Rose, whose family were all in the Bahamas, showed up just as we were walking into the kitchen, which was probably good since it split the attention between Rose, whom the family loved, and Wanda. Wanda was looking a bit traumatized, although still smiling. My family is very friendly and outgoing...maybe overwhelmingly so. It had even taken some of the spouses a while to get used to the collective turmoil that erupted when we were all together. My wife, Lou, had been much different from me: loud, funny, and the life of the party. Wanda leaned on (supportive) Rose for a while and then was swept into the chaos. I'd never seen

Wanda have a drink before. She accepted a glass of wine as Rose did. I was relieved. I hadn't really been worried because I knew my family would just accept, almost as if there was nothing even the least bit unusual, Wanda and Marsh. Within minutes everybody had individually come up and said hi to Wanda, introducing themselves, and we were all one big gang.

When Allegra, the last to introduce herself to Wanda, came up and gave her a hug, Wanda looked at me over her shoulder and raised her eyebrows. I nodded. We shared a smile.

In our family, the adults all draw names to see who gives another adult a present. They each draw a kid's name as well and each kid draws an adult and one of the other kids. The kids can't buy anything, the gift must be hand-made (with a little help from the parents of the younger ones). There is some competition about who can make the best gift.

After a good deal of adult Christmas cheer and snacks, everyone having to yell to be heard above the din, we have the kids come up and we all gather in the living room. The kids exchange their gifts first, including one from the parent who drew his or her name and vice versa.

Then they open mine, which they enjoy because they know they'll be getting something unusual. I, as the only present grandparent, buy a little something for each grandchild. I spend quite a bit of time trying to find a unique gift that they might be surprised by. No clothes. Nowadays kids pretty much get what they wanted the moment they want it. At least kids in families like ours. And, of course, I had little idea what they want fashion-wise. It hit me how gratuitous all these gifts might appear to Wanda and Marsh.

Since none of the in-law's parents have a family as large as ours, they all agreed to give us Christmas Eve, and they got Christmas Day. So, the kids open their presents, we eat, then the kids once again disappear down into their realm, and we adults exchange our draws.

So, when Lizzie yelled down that it was time to open presents, Allegra headed down apparently to encourage them to rise to the occasion. Though this occasion might be the only time the kids actually come when they're called. The adults all headed into the cathedral-ceilinged living room, where the at least twelve-foot tree loomed, to await the stampede.

I had noticed Wanda glance several times toward the downstairs doorway, probably hoping Marshawn would surface, alive, from the depths. But—no Marshawn, even after most of the thundering herd had emerged. I was watching Wanda when they all came rushing up, and saw her eyes open wide. I turned and carrying Marsh was Allegra. I'm not sure why, but I immediately choked up. Golden brown Allegra carrying shiny black Marshawn was almost too much for me.

I looked back at Wanda and she was looking at me. She smiled and nodded. I wasn't sure exactly why she was nodding, but I nodded back.

The kids all scurried to the tree, grabbing and handing their gift to the name they had drawn. The adults all took their turns meeting Marsh. He was handed off from one adult to another. He looked a bit stunned but smiled the entire time. As we settled around the tree, it hit me…stupid, ignorant me: I hadn't thought to include Marsh in the kids' drawing. What an idiot. Until Hadley, my oldest daughter's daughter—a very observant, compassionate person—noticed my panic and saved me. She suggested that they pick straws to see who would get to give their gift to Marshawn. Well, there I went choking up again. I saw a couple of the younger boys thinking, 'Hmm. I'm not so sure about this.' But with everyone else cheering Hadley's suggestion, what could they do? I interjected that I had a gift for Marshawn, so nobody had to forfeit getting a present, but I was booed down. Everyone now, even the younger boys, started chanting, "Marshawn; Marshawn!"

Marsh sat on the floor, not by me or his mother, looking around, eyes wide, at all the kids as they chanted his name. When it quieted down, Marsh pointed at Sadie, Abby and Abe's daughter, who was also almost three, and in his deep little voice said, "I want her gift." His voice cracked everybody up. I knew my family was going to love Marshawn, and he would love them. Cool for Marsh; cool for us.

When I suggested that maybe he should get one of the boys' gift, he gave me his bad-ass stare and slowly shook his head.

Sadie walked over to Mac and Hiball's daughter, Abileen, who had initially been the recipient of Sadie's gift, and Abilene happily handed it over. Sadie padded slowly over to Marsh and stood looking down at him, serious, not smiling, not reaching to hand him the gift. The room went silent. I, and apparently everyone in the room, was engrossed in anticipation. Marsh shuffled to his feet and looked expectantly at Sadie, as if this was some unrehearsed ritual. I had no idea what either was thinking. It was so quiet you could hear the tinsel's fragile rattle on the tree. Finally, Sadie tentatively reached out as if to hand the gift to Marsh. Then, of course, Marsh didn't reach for it. I looked at Wanda. She was watching intently, looking a bit worried. Everyone held their breath, even Randi who was only six months, didn't make a sound. The suspense was palpable. To this day I wonder what was going on in their little heads.

Finally, Sadie said, "Here. Take it. It's yours."

Marsh accepted the gift. It was not terribly large and looked light, but Marsh sat back down, laid the gift in his lap, and looked up at Sadie. Sadie looked down at Marsh for a moment and finally said, "Open it."

The present was in a colorful gift bag with red tissue paper sticking out the top. Marsh peeked in, trying to see what the devil was in the bag. Sadie sat down next to him, took the bag from Marsh, and tore out a doll Sadie's mother, Abby, had made—a girl in a swimsuit with stickers stuck all over her. A little gasp escaped from all the adults, except Abby and Abe of course, when we all saw that the girl doll was brown. Marsh looked questionably at Sadie, and she said, "They're tattoos."

I'm sure everybody, like me, wondered what, exactly, Marsh would think of a girl doll, brown, loaded with tattoos. A smile came to his face, his hand holding the doll shot up in the air, and he yelled, much louder than I've ever heard him, before or since, "Yea!"

Tension escaped like we all had a slow leak. We all clapped. I looked at Wanda, who had her hand over her heart. Her eyes slid toward me, noticeably exhaled…and she smiled.

After the gift exchange and the din of dinner, the kids once again vanished rapidly. I had given Marsh a new book and he had tossed me a brief, but knowing, smile, before being once again swept away. The adults all refreshed their glasses and settled in with their presents back in the living room. There's a dollar limit on what we each can spend, and some competition here, too, about who comes up with either the funniest or coolest present, or best bang for the buck. I had had the foresight to rearrange Wanda as my draw. I figured the present she had along was for me…so, copasetic. She insisted that I open mine from her first when it was our time to open. When I tore the paper off, I was shocked. It was a book. Not in itself surprising. But what did surprise me is that it was a hard-cover copy of *My Life and Hard Times* by James Thurber. Now, I already had the book because Thurber is one of my favorite authors, favorite humorous for sure. I was totally astounded. Even though a writers' award for humorous fiction is called the Thurber Award, I've found very few people know of him. He's certainly not mainstream. He is hysterical…if you like wry, dry humor. How did she know this? She was becoming more and more of a mystery. I glanced at Rose, but she was looking very unsuspicious. "We're reading this together," I yelled over to Wanda, and I thought I saw her eyes water up.

I had bought her a smartphone. I knew she wanted one. All her cousins had one. Wanda felt she couldn't afford it. As I found out that first night in a chilly house, Wanda was frugal. When she opened it, she paused a moment, then looked up at me briefly. I wasn't sure what she was thinking, but she had to wipe her eyes. So, I figured: good?

On the way home, Wanda was just as talkative as on the way there, asking more questions about each of my kids and grandkids, especially Allegra. Marshawn kept trying to talk but couldn't get a word in edgewise. Suddenly, a remarkable bellow from such a small person catapulted around the car. Wanda froze mid-sentence and I looked at Marsh in the rearview mirror. After a moment of silence, Marshawn stated: "I liked them. They were nice. And they're smart."

Woow, I thought. A kid that age that recognizes 'smart' has gotta be pretty darn smart himself. Yes, sir. Smart himself.

CHAPTER 7

Things were good after Christmas. We seemed to be almost settling into a routine. We'd go to the daycare group every Thursday and I'd come over on Mondays. Wanda even started having me for dinner on occasion. "Having pity on the old bachelor," she'd say. We'd take turns reading. Marsh usually in my lap when I read now, following along, mouthing the words as I read. He started to visually recognize some words and I found a simple little book of pictures with words I thought he'd recognize, and we would try to get him to read it aloud. My heart was full. I mean all my kids and grandkids had sat on my lap when I read to them. Did I feel that…proud, satisfied then as I did now? No matter. What's the difference?

Marsh usually went to bed easily. Not sure why—none of my kids had. It had always been an ordeal with excuses and required rituals attempting to delay the inevitable. It looked like most of my kids' kids were following suit. Serves em right. Marshawn would hug me goodnight regularly now—there's that heart thing again—and Wanda'd lay him down and I'd never hear a peep. Marshawn and Wanda seemed to have this strong connection, understanding, between them.

The first Monday after Christmas, after Marsh had gone to bed, I pulled out Wanda's *My Life and Hard Times*. I was a little reticent reading Thurber with Wanda. I mean his humor is quite dry and esoteric and, well…set in a pretty antiquated White culture. Not that I thought Wanda wasn't intelligent. She was, I had happily realized. But I guess Thurber is too subtle for most folks. But when I had thought about it, Wanda rather had Thurber's dry wit. Like the first night, asking me if I was afraid of her…and then smiling. Not a cruel smile, but a knowing one. And I *had* been afraid of her, and she was just letting me know she was aware of it. Put us on the same level, somehow. And the nursing/boob-popping-out thing and telling Billy he had a skinny ass. I was so worried about everything that first night, I was more shocked or whatever at the time, and so didn't see the humor. Now, looking back, I think it's hilarious. She's always asking me if I know how 'ignorant' I am. And she's right—I can be a total dumbass. Anyway, I was curious as hell to see her reaction to Thurber.

My Life and Hard Times is a series of snippets relating to the same eccentric family but in no order. Random droll recollections by Thurber. The first snippet I picked was "The Dog that Bit People." It had always cracked me up. It was not slap-stick or gut-funny, but Thurber had a hilarious way of understating things—which *is*, of course, more subtle. But the dry understatements had a way of building momentum. By the time I got to: "…But the Airedale, as I have said, was the worst of all my dogs…a big burly choleric dog, he always acted as if he thought I wasn't one of the family. There was a slight advantage in being one of the family, for he didn't bite the family as often as he bit strangers…" we were both laughing hysterically, including at his primitively simplistic yet outrageously humorous sketches.

Before I started reading again, Wanda shushed me. We could hear Marshawn laughing in his room. Wanda and I looked at each other with eyebrows raised. After our next outbreak of laughter, we listened again…and sure enough, he was laughing like crazy. Naturally, I had another little heart-leap. He was laughing at us laughing. I almost wanted to believe he could hear me reading and also thought Thurber was amusing.

When I was done reading, we both collapsed on the back of the sofa, exhausted from laughing so hard. A thought seized my memory: when my wife and I went to bed and wanted to have fun without the labor of love-making—well not "labor" exactly, but you know what I mean—we'd read Thurber aloud and I could feel a bond more subtle but almost as close: laughing, soulfully, until we cried. Reading Thurber and laughing together with Wanda I felt was creating a bond, a bond that I knew couldn't and didn't have any ill intentions or stirring of temptations. Although I felt like I was growing to love Wanda and Marsh, I felt like I was reading to my granddaughter and relishing in the laughter of my great-grand-son. The way it must be for this amazing program to work. I did wonder at the danger of feeling like Wanda and Marsh were… like family. Getting too close. Is it possibly unwise to get too close to someone? My wife, Louise, dying, was…I don't know. I mean is it the stronger the love the greater the loss? I dealt with it alright, I guess. And I know that I'm not the first one to have had to deal with death of a spouse, but one day she was there, next she was gone. Gone? What the hell is 'gone?' No more reading Thurber, although when I'd think of us, I'd still laugh lightly to myself until I inevitably cried. What if something were to cause Wanda and Marsh to be gone? Not dead, but out of my life? That could indeed happen. Would likely happen eventually, although I, right now, could not imagine it. Man! Well, gotta keep perspective. I'm here for them. Not the other way around.

Marsh's third birthday came before I knew it. I thought it would be cool to bring my kids and grandkids to the Deasels' garage, assuming that would once again be the venue. When I mentioned it to Wanda a while ago, she said she'd talk to them. They did talk about it and decided they liked the idea. They said bring Rose and Billy, too.

The younger of my twins, Edie, her husband, Tad, and their two boys weren't going to be able to make it. They would be on vacation in Costa Rica, but everyone else, except for Chris and Lizzy's two oldest who were away at college, were available and up for it.

My family all came to my house first and we decided to caravan the fifteen of us in three cars. I couldn't believe how excited everybody was. The grandkids, ranging in age from one to sixteen, couldn't wait to see Marshawn again. It was almost like he was one of their cousins. My own kids are always up for adventures and had liked Wanda and, naturally, Marsh…so they were just as excited as their kids.

I had decided not to say too much about what to expect. Just enough to get the suspense going. I had just told them they would be surprised. I didn't even tell them it was a garage we were going to. I hadn't even given them the address because with their technology stuff, they'd probably find a photo of the place.

I finally had to tell them the address when we were leaving my house—in case we got separated. Of course, as soon as my son, Christopher, who I was riding with—including his wife, Lizzy, their sixteen-year-old twins, Jax and Maci, and Allegra and I in their huge Suburban—got in the car, he pulled up the address on his dash thingy—big as a TV screen and said: "Oh, wow. That's just off Broadway. An interesting part of town. Cool." The adventure was on.

On the way there I was told by the twins, Jax and Maci, that Marsh had really taken a liking to Sadie, Abby and Abe's three-year-old. The twins both talked about how protective Marsh had been of Sadie. It reaffirmed for me that Marsh may have experienced D'jerk abusing his mother. Consequently, along with being the keeper of the little girls in our group, Marsh would be a knight in shining armor for all women, including Sadie. Maci said that when play got a little rough, he also stayed close to Randi, Ade and Andy's one year old. I was proud.

When we pulled up to the Deasels' garage, Chris said: "This is the address. What is it? A garage?"

"Yup," I answered. 'The Deasel Bros. and Big Sis.'"

"Cool," he said again. Everyone else was quiet, surveying the unexpected locale.

The other two cars pulled up right next to us. I noticed Billy and Rose's cars were already there. We all got out, everyone was pensive, also perusing the scene. There were still cars and bikes everywhere. Mac, my eldest daughter, finally asked, "Is this where we're going, Dad?"

Suddenly the garage office door flew open, and out rushed Marsh. All the kids ran to him and there were semi-hugs, high fives, low fives, knucks…and I'm not shittin' ya, but Sadie had kept her distance from the commotion of the older kids. So, Marsh walked over and gave her a huge hug. My heart, once again—well, you know. I didn't even mind not getting a hug, much less recognition, myself.

I was dying of curiosity to see how everyone would react meeting a hoard of giants. But once inside, the grandkids said hi to the Deasels, unfazed, and followed Marsh right to a fire truck squatting in the closest bay. Marsh immediately climbed right up. The grands looked around for approval and the Deasels all roared. Lee yelled, "Go ahead. Get up on that there fire truck." Within seconds there were kids crawling all over the vehicle. I thought great coincidence that it happened to be in the shop. But when I asked later about it, Lee told me they brought it in to make Marshawn proud and to keep the kids all busy. Smart.

Well, it was a riot. With the poor acoustics in the garage and the kids' chaos, you could hardly hear yourself think, louder even than Chris and Lizzie's kitchen. The Deas's didn't have big lungs for nothing. And my kids are all outgoing, except for Allegra. She was a good conversationalist, one-on-one, but not as raucous as her brother and sisters. She and Rose appeared to be soulmates, as they stood off a lot, chatting quietly. They looked like sisters. Billie, who is a great guy, mixed with everybody. I noticed Marsh staying close to Sadie. Cool. Wanda was a little subdued, I also noticed. But it was quite the birthday party. All cool—so I thought.

CHAPTER 8

My family talked about this get-together all year until Marsh's fourth birthday. Problem was, it was a tough year for Wanda and me.

Wanda had *texted* me, on her new phone of course, right after Marsh's birthday, not to come for our Monday meeting and that she couldn't make the Thursday evening group session. I checked with Ona, my friend from daycare, and she told me Wanda had been dropping Marsh off for daycare. I was almost sorry I'd given her the smartphone, with her ability to text. Without actually speaking to somebody, hearing inflection, emotion, etc. in a voice, and not being able to ask questions, only a limited amount of actual communication happens in a frickin' text. Actually, no real communication—only information. I guess people tend to think adding emojis is emotion or something…but that's total bull. I immediately texted—a good use of texting in this case—Rose to call me when she had a chance.

She called that night. When I asked, she told me she hadn't talked to Wanda since Marsh's birthday party…that at the party she also had felt Wanda *was* a little offish. But, with all the chaos, that would be understandable. And Rose expressed rather fervently that she had spent a lot of time talking to Allegra and had found her very interesting…that she really liked her. As I said, I had noticed. Cool, I thought.

When I brought up the possibility of a new boyfriend, Rose said Wanda had not confided anything of the sort to her and that that was the downside of me having shown up with her at Wanda's house regarding the Dejon circumstance. That even though Rose hadn't broken a confidence, it may have appeared that way. Rose said she absolutely would not call Wanda and report back to me if a new guy was in the picture. That Wanda would never trust her again if she did. That I should just deal with it myself.

I wasn't angry with Rose; she was right, as usual. I just wasn't sure if Wanda would be honest with me…if she even responded. Something was obviously up. To be safe I texted her: "Was there a problem?" When I didn't get an answer back, I guessed it was a new guy. Everything had been so good; I couldn't imagine what else it could be. I figured I'd just show up on Monday. I wanted to deal with this before it escalated.

Just as I was heading to bed to read, and get my mind off Wanda, the phone rang. To my surprise it was Lee. My opinion of Lee had only grown. She was a strong, straight-shooting, well-endowed woman, and, surprisingly, I found her, although somewhat intimidating, quite captivating. I mean, let's face it: I had never met a woman that came even close to being as much 'woman,' as Lee.

What almost knocked me out of my penny loafers, was one time I mentioned to Rose I wondered why Lee never brought a guy around. I assumed she must have had guys interested…or else scared them away. Rose, reminiscent of Wanda, had rolled her eyes and told me how oblivious I was. "She's gay, you fool."

I was shocked, of course, but had asked why she didn't bring her…lady friend…partner, whatever, along? I never know what the words are for anything but hetero, married relationships. You know…like 'husband and wife.' I was indeed a straight, traditional, middle-class bore who drives an extremely practical Corolla. Boring, conservative, and obviously oblivious. I mean, occasionally, I'd see some guys that act like a couple and so I'd assume they were homosexual…well, alright: gay. Somebody told me I was supposed to say 'queer' now. I could never do that. With women, I admit I have no clue. Proven further when Rose told me Lee's friend had been at the gatherings. "What?!" I had exclaimed. "Who?"

"Colleen," she had answered. "Colleen!" I expounded. "Colleen flirted with me at both of Marsh's birthday parties." I could feel her eyes rolling without looking at her. She condescended to tell me that, like most guys, I assumed being 'friendly' was flirting. That "maybe she was a little 'coy' with Marshawn's advocate because…because she's not interested in you 'that way,' and so could."

OK, I admit to being the fool. I didn't deny it. But back to Lee: when I had asked her what was up, she told me that if I indicated to Wanda anything about what she was going to tell me, she'd break my neck. And I believed her. There was, she said, a new guy in the picture—Ed. That he seemed a good guy. Not like Tremain, apparently her ex-husband's name, or Dejon. He was college educated and had a good job. Treated Wanda well, so far, and Marshawn seemed to accept him.

She also informed me: "You know, you have been good for Wanda. Both Marsh's father and Dejon had been losers. Street niggers." (This made me cringe. Something I'd never say…but then I'm not Black). "Maybe good," she continued, "for…carnal exploration, but that was about it."

'Carnal exploration!?' That was one of the cleverest euphemisms for 'sex' that I had ever heard.

"Wanda definitely has more self-confidence now," Lee continued. "She wants her next guy to be good for Marsh. She worries what you will think, too, you know."

"She worries what I think?" I had responded.

"Of course," I could feel her rolling her eyes. I was beginning to get an eye-rolling complex. "She knows you've been good for Marshawn. She also realizes you've been good for her. She likes and trusts you. She's worried what you'll think about Ed."

"Well, he sounds…pretty darn good."

"Darn?" Lee laughed. "Man, you are a honky."

"That bad?" I asked, for some reason not really offended. I mean—I was a simple 'honky.'

Lee laughed harder. "No, not bad. You're just the only person I know that'd say 'darn.' No, you're real, man… and darn OK," she said and laughed again. "I like you. I'm glad you're here. So, sit down and have a chat with Ed."

"Well, why is Wanda avoiding me? It wouldn't seem like she's wanting me to meet Ed. She's canceled both our Monday and the Thursday group meetings."

"Put yourself in her shoes, man. First of all, Ed seems like a decent guy, but you think he's happy that Marshawn…and Wanda…like you?"

"*Like* me?" I said. "'Like' me like…you realize I think of Wanda as a granddaughter. Marsh as a great-grandson."

"I know, I know, for shit's sake. She doesn't 'like' you that way, either. Men! But she feels close to you, and so does Marsh. Suppose that doesn't make Ed a little defensive? Wanda's caught in the middle. She's scared."

"Scared?" I interjected. "Scared of what?"

"Put yourself in her shoes, for shit's sake. Are all men really this stupid?"

I laughed. "Probably. I guess I'm scared too."

"What the hell you scared of?"

"Look, Lee. I'm afraid I've gotten awfully attached to Marshawn…well, Wanda, too. I'd have a hard time if they were to exit my life now.

"Look. Be there Monday. I'm afraid she might still try to avoid facing the situation, but I'll make sure they're both there. You and Ed work things out. How's that?"

Great. I wasn't wild about that proposition but said, "Thanks, Lee. You know you should work on people, not cars."

She laughed. She had a great, full deep-throated laugh. It sounded both gentle and tough. Like a tap on your nose from a knuckle. "I'll stick with cars," she said. "Cars can be fixed. You be there Monday."

"Oh, I will."

I drove up and parked in front of the house. It was late February, but a light rain was falling and oddly thunder was growling in the distance. Unusual for Minneapolis in the winter, making this part of the world a dangerous place to drive or even walk. I slip-slided up to the house realizing I was holding my breath. Lee wouldn't tell me anything more about Ed—said to "Man up and just deal with it, fool." So, I had no idea, really, what to expect. And I was worried. If it weren't for Marsh—and Wanda, of course—I would have retreated. It was, or had been, in my nature to avoid conflict. I certainly wasn't comfortable confronting it.

I cautiously walked up the front steps, but when I knocked, there was no response. It was getting dark, but no lights were on in the house. Was she hiding in there? If she was, were Ed and Marshawn hiding as well? I thought that'd be weird. So, should I take a hint and leave? I took a deep breath and pounded on the door. Although apprehensive, I felt I needed to face the situation. When there was still no response, I pounded even harder. Sill no response. Now what? Do I go peek in windows? Knock on the back door? Both of those seemed stupid, but I decided to look in the garage to see if her car was there. It was, but so what? She'd probably be with Ed and it sounded like he'd certainly have a car. As I was walking back out front toward my car, a 'Deasel Bros.' wrecker pulled up. Lee got out but I could see Wanda in the rider's seat. Then Marsh's face pushed up against the back window. His breath clouded the window, and when I waved, I wasn't sure he could see me.

Lee walked over, hood up, smiling sheepishly. I was afraid to ask what was going on. "She won't talk to you," Lee said simply.

I was at a loss and felt almost panicky, unable to say anything. An ominous knot was tying up my gut. I wasn't sure I even wanted to know what was going on and why it was that Wanda wouldn't talk to me.

"She's stubborn. Always has been. When she was little, she'd go days without talking. You couldn't make her."

"Why?" was all I said. I wasn't sure if I meant 'why wouldn't she talk to me?' or 'why was she so over-the top stubborn?'

Lee raised her eyebrows: "Why what?"

I didn't answer.

"Look, Ed's upset. He doesn't want to talk to you, either."

"I thought he wouldn't even know I was coming?"

Lee shook her head. "I felt I had to tell her you were going to show up. She hasn't done this damn stubborn crap for a while. Kinda surprises me." Lee stood tall, taking a deep breath. Her bearing always gave me a little jolt. "She won't talk to me either."

OK. What to do? Just leave? That would be the easiest. What I would normally do. I wanted to go over to the tow truck and say something 'special.' Make a great little speech that would fix everything. But I knew I wasn't going to do that.

When I looked back toward the tow truck, Marsh had rubbed his hand in circles, clearing the window. He looked sad and made a little wave to me. I wanted to cry. I was mad at myself. "Screw it," I said, looking at Lee, who raised her eyebrows, and I walked over to the truck. I could see Wanda watching me out of the corner of her eye. Her face passive, expressionless. I ignored her and put my nose up against Marsh's window and he pressed his nose against the window opposite mine. He smiled, his eyes not looking happy though.

"I'll see you Thursday" I yelled. "I've got a new book to show you."

He looked toward Wanda and I could see him mouthing, "Maaa." I looked and could see the side of Wanda's face and could tell it remained a stone. Marsh came back to the window, put his hands against the glass, and nodded, putting his nose against the glass again, but he must have been holding his breath before, because it clouded up right away and his face disappeared. I tapped my knuckles against where his nose was and yelled: "Thursday."

When I turned away, Lee was standing there with her arms folded, slowly shaking her head. She walked to me, pulled my head to her, somewhere between what must have been her breasts as she was a good foot taller than me, rubbed her knuckles against my wet scalp, not terribly gentle, and said: "You're OK for a White boy. Be patient." She got in the truck, and as they drove away, Marsh cleared his window again and waved.

I couldn't even wave back. Wanda was sitting there staring straight ahead. I was scared. I'd cry if I wasn't a frickin' Norwegian.

So, Thursday came and with considerable trepidation I headed toward Wanda's, driving slowly, feeling like a little kid who had climbed up and toddled out onto a high dive. Wanted to turn around but couldn't. There were people behind expecting me to do something. There was no turning back. I had to take the leap.

When I pulled up front of Wanda's, there, sitting on the front step, was a dark Asian-looking man. The rain had abated but the clouds were hanging low. The cold had stayed north, and it was still unusually mild for a Minnesota winter. The meager snow crusty and a dirty white. I hesitated in my car but decided I had to face the music no matter the tune. So, I walked up to him as confidently as I could, stuck out my hand, and choked out: "Hello. You must be Ed. I'm Ryan."

He looked at my hand, looked up. Didn't smile. I kept my hand out and smiled the best I could. Finally, he stood and took my hand...and shook it I wouldn't say warmly. Whew. I didn't think he would hit me, but it had appeared he wasn't going to shake my hand.

"I know who you are, of course," he said a little unpleasantly. "Correct me if I'm wrong, but Wanda said she made it clear she wasn't going to your little 'gathering.'" From his sarcasm I could tell, number one, he wasn't dumb, and two, he didn't think much of our Thursday 'gatherings.'

"So...she's talking now?"

He let a little grin slip out. "A little."

"Can we talk?" I asked. Then an idea struck me. "Does Marsh want to go? You know, if she expects daycare pro bono, she and Marsh must attend the Thursday 'gatherings,' as you put it?"

He hesitated, sat back down, and said, "As a matter of fact he does want to go."

"Well then, why don't you and I take him? You can check out our little gathering." I was surprising myself. I'm sure I wouldn't have been so gutsy—for me, not running was gutsy—if it weren't for Marshawn.

He flinched and raised his eyebrows. "What?"

I didn't repeat myself. He was just buying time because he was taken by surprise.

"I don't really belong there, though. Do I?" he finally said.

"Oh, yes, if you want to be involved in Marshawn's life. And you'll understand what it's all about if you come along."

"Hmm. What about Wanda?"

"She doesn't want to come, let her stay home and talk to herself."

He smiled. "Well…"

"You do realize that if Wanda wants daycare for Marsh, they *have* to attend the Thursday meetings?"

"But you don't have to be involved. I can take your place. Maybe with me in the picture, Wanda can stay home and take care of Marsh, herself. Not have to work. Not be tied to the daycare deal."

"Oh. I see. The relationship must be moving along rather quickly? Is there a ring involved?" I didn't want to alienate him, but it almost seemed like this was a contest to him. He had only been dating Wanda for less than a month…as far as I knew.

This got a hard stare from Ed. "Look," I said, "I hope to hell you two make it. Lee—you've met Lee?"

He nodded.

"Lee said some good things about you. Said you've been good to Marsh. Great. You think I've been bad for Marsh?"

He stretched his legs out, leaned back on his elbows, and gazed at me.

"Well?"

"No," he finally said, rather grudgingly, shaking his head.

"You know most kids without fathers have behavior problems and do poorly in school?"

"You're not his father."

"You either," I challenged. I couldn't help getting a little defensive. "Until that happens, I think it's good for Marshawn to have an advocate in his life."

"An 'advocate' huh?"

"You know what I mean."

"How about I be this 'advocate'?" he said, smiling.

"Great. Two advocates are better than one," I came back with. "Do I threaten you?"

He sat back up but didn't answer.

"Look," I said, and sat next to him on the stoop. "Let's go to this gathering, which is not a bad word for it. I think you'll see that it's very good for Marsh. Good for Wanda, too."

"Oh?" he said, buying time again and gazing out at our cars.

Not far from my old Corolla, I now noticed, was a new, flashier Corolla. "Nice car," I said. "Let's take a ride in it."

He looked at me and back out at our cars. I waited. He didn't say anything for what seemed like an eternity. Finally: "I'm not sure what Wanda will think of this."

"Like I said, let her stay home and mull it over. What she won't like is not being there. She's quite the social butterfly," I said and winked at him. What the wink was about, I had no idea. I'd never winked at anybody in my life. What an idiot.

He looked back out toward the cars. "Well, let's get Marsh's car seat in my car, then."

I couldn't hold back a sigh of relief. Believe me, this little negotiation was brazen for me. But…I won.

He smiled at my sigh and said, "You better wait out here."

"Gladly," I responded. "You won't be sorry."

After a few moments, Marsh came ambling out the door bundled up. I stood and picked him up off the stoop, got a good hug, and set him down.

As we headed toward Ed's car, Ed following with the car seat, I saw Wanda come up to the screen door, the inside door open. Although her face was shadowed by the screen, I swear I could see her eyes glowing. I knew that glare would be there. I stopped and gave her a quick little wave but got no response. Marsh shuffled slowly but determinedly, his chubby little legs wide apart. I figured it was going to be interesting establishing a relationship with Ed.

But all in all, I didn't dislike him. He certainly was an improvement from what I'd heard about D'jerk.

When we got to the 'gathering,' a little late, Marsh plodded over to a group of kids sitting at a table working on something. Ona's daughter, tall for her age and, as I've said, tall and demure like her mother, was at the table. Marsh and Remmi had become friends. They were about the same age and would more than likely be in the same class in kindergarten. Marsh high-fived Remmi, also Pat—Mick and Patty's son—and Benji, wide and roly-poly like her mother, Deloria.

Shahlla, a new, young Iranian aid, greeted Marsh and gave him a hug, then settled Marsh into whatever it was the group of now six was doing.

Heather, who had stuck around even if the pay was crap, had the other kids in a corner reading a story to them.

The parents and other advocates were milling around a large table looking at some new book arrivals and trading others.

Ed perused the scene, his eyebrows raised, lips pursed, and slowly nodding his head—I hoped in approval. On the drive, Marsh and I had told him the names of the kids. I had been surprised that Marsh knew the names of all the parents and most of the advocates, as well. Ed hadn't said anything, but seemed to be absorbing the names he wouldn't, of course, remember.

His eyes, now, settled on both Ona, who, being taller than everyone and striking in appearance, stood out, and Asia who was talking to her.

I noticed and told him Asia was the teacher. Ona was the first to notice us, gave us her electric smile, and waved. I waved back and walked Ed over to introduce him to Asia. All the adults were so engrossed in the books and chatting so excitedly, they didn't notice us, at first.

Finally, Asia asked for attention, laid her hand on Ed's shoulder and introduced him, saying cleverly that he was here in Wanda's absence. I couldn't help noticing a catch in the way Ed and Asia looked a second and third time at each other. Well, they were both at least partly Asian, so that must be it, I told myself.

When I looked up to Ona, I could see she caught something, too. I felt like Ona and I connected well. I thought it a weird quirk of fate that when the woman is a lot taller than the admiring man—me in this case—a relationship almost seems out of the question. With Ona at near six feet and me at a middling five eight…that four inches seems insurmountable. I'd love to ask her out, especially now since her flannel-wearing boyfriend from the north woods had gone back to his forest. Of course, she was also a lot younger than I was—so, two probably insurmountable barriers made a 'union' unlikely. But, Lord, was she adorable.

Everything was moving along quite smoothly—Ed was a little stand-offish but mixed pretty well and was smiling—until the door opened and slammed shut loud enough to get everyone's attention. To my surprise in walked Wanda. Her eyes caught mine and she stomped directly over to me. She stepped close—in my 'personal space'—and hands on hips stared hard at me. I smiled, more out of fear than anything, and she put a fist up to my chin. I had no idea what was in her eyes—I doubt she knew, either, but there definitely was a…fierceness I guess I'd say. Ona, whom I had a hard time not hanging with and so was next to me, leaned down and asked Wanda if there was something the matter.

Wanda looked up at Ona, said sharply, "Hi, Ona. I can't decide."

Ed was soon at her side, but she turned away and looked for Marsh. All the kids, well everybody, had stopped what they were doing at the 'slam' and were focusing rapt attention on Wanda…and me, I guess. When her eyes met Marsh's, he gave her a little wave. She waved back and looked at the entire quizzical group, all frozen in their position since the time of the dramatic entrance. Books were still in the hands of the adults in startled anticipation. Wanda's fist was still at my chin. She glared, of course, at me, made a very animal-like grunt, lowered her fist, and smiled sheepishly at the room. "Hey, Wanda," "What's up," and "Everything OK?" tentatively floated about. Of course, I had no idea what they were thinking about me and what I might have done to precipitate the drama. So, I just shrugged my shoulders and smiled sheepishly.

She looked passively at Ed, threw a quick little glare again at me—nothing new—and walked over and started talking to everyone. Laughter was soon accompanying her. Ed had a wide-eyed look on his face, his mouth partially open. I whispered to him: "I told you. She's a social butterfly. The life of this party."

He looked at me, back at her, just as a burst of laughter exploded. "I...I never. I've never seen that side of her."

I wasn't sure which 'side' he meant...the irascible or jocular. "Only two places, as far as I know, she feels comfortable enough to percolate," I told him, "is here and with the Deasels."

I poked him and pointed to Marsh, who was giggling at a table with a Jew, a White Irish kid, a Black kid, and a Hispanic kid. When Ed looked back to me, I raised my eyebrows.

He nodded.

CHAPTER 9

January and well into February had remained quite warm. After the February rain trickery, the winter returned from its pilgrimage north full force, bringing with it a ton of snow as well as wind. In Minnesota, if you're gonna have cold, you best have snow so you have something to enjoy outside. Of course, the wind is the fiercest adversary and real culprit for ruining an outing.

I had given Marsh a little orange plastic sled in hopes of flying down sliding hills with him tucked safely between my knees, or at least winter walks pulling Marsh through the snow. Unfortunately, Wanda told me she was warm-blooded, hated the cold, and so hadn't had an occasion to utilize the sled, yet. Then once, Marsh let it slip that Ed had taken him sledding on *my* sled. As soon as he said it, he looked sad, probably mimicking the look that immediately caught in my eye. But rather than be sad myself, I quickly decided to cheer myself that Marshawn was learning, I suppose you'd say—empathy. He was really becoming a good, sensitive kid.

Ed only made a few of the Thursday-night gatherings but was there every Monday for our reading night. He seemed to support the importance of Marsh being read to and we all took turns reading aloud. Marsh now usually sat in Ed's lap, but when it was my turn, he'd crawl over and settle in like old times. Speaking of old times, I really missed reading Thurber with Wanda. She was, again, not unfriendly toward me. But a little distance had grown, and a little warmth dwindled. But, of course, I understood. The friendliest times were on our drive to the gatherings when Ed wasn't along. Marsh was turning into a little goof, much like his mother, and seemed to sense the old comfortable comradery missing between us, and so always managed to get us laughing.

Then, the Monday before Marsh's fourth birthday, Ed was absent. Wanda, unusual for her, had been a little, what I'd call, almost giggly. Unusual for her, with me at least. After we'd read and she'd put Marsh to bed, she plopped down on the couch right next to me, brushed against my arm and shoulder—something she'd never do with Ed around—and smiled mischievously. She had been hiding something behind her back. Then, suddenly, with a flash of show, she held a book up to my face almost proudly: *Is Sex Necessary? Or, Why You Feel the Way You Do.*

OK, I knew it was a novelette by Thurber. Again, I had it already. Even a drab, balding Corolla-driver had to take advantage of this opportunity. "Really!?" I said, doing my best to act shocked. "Well, I'm a little taken aback. A little risqué wouldn't you say? What would Marsh think…much less Ed?"

She lowered the book and blushed. I wasn't sure I knew what a Black person blushing would look like. But this was definitely a blush. "It's Thurber you fool!" she shouted and hit me with the book.

I couldn't help but smile and she screamed and hit me, again. So, I grabbed the book from her before she decided she was having fun, and read, aloud, the review of the book on the back cover by *Saturday Review:* "One of the silliest books I've read in years, and perfectly lovely. It left this reviewer weak, partially paralyzed, with a writhen face streaming with tears."

She smiled at me and said, "Why do you suppose we cry when we are amused?"

Now a couple things: first—when I met Wanda, she not only didn't appear amused, but I doubt she had ever used the word. Now it rolled off her tongue so naturally. It dawned on me that by reading to Marsh, not only was he developing vocabulary as well as a sense of humor, but so was Wanda. Second—I would say that Thurber was a master of what you might recall: 'The Understatement.' And that, as I've said, fits quite naturally into the sensibilities of a Norwegian...since most—at least one for sure—live understated lives. But a single Black mother living in an impoverished city neighborhood? It made me wonder what is lost and glossed over by living and growing up in an uninspiring environment. And what wit and intelligence can become untethered by only a little catalyst. I mean, can reading stories to kids unleash the imagination in an adult as well? I'd say Wanda disproved the idiom 'you can't teach an old dog new tricks.' Are those tricks buried there in all of us who are stagnated for some reason in some way by circumstance?

I mean I'd handed a copy of *My Life and Hard Times* to many a college graduate—one, for example, lugging a PhD along with his briefcase—thinking they would call me gasping for air the next morning, tears streaming onto their smartphones. When I didn't hear back, I'd called and asked, "Well, waddya think?"

"Think about what?"

"*My Life and Hard Times*," I'd exclaimed, exasperated.

"Oh, yeah. Well, I started it... He doesn't draw very well, does he?"

At that, I'd given up. I mean Wanda got the humor! She and I would laugh so hard, if not harder, at his insane little humorous (yes, Mr. PhD, drawn intentionally minimal and simplistic) sketches, than at his ingenious written understatings. (The cartoon sketches are understated, too, you unimaginative doctor of bland.)

If they let me (I know Thurber himself would give me permission if he was still kickin'), I'd show you an example of one of his sketches. If one does not appear here and you like this excerpt from the first paragraph of the "Preface" to *Is Sex Necessary?*, you'll just have to go out and fork over the price of one of his rather brief (but ample) books. If you don't like the excerpt, I'll just assume you're Swedish and have no sense of humor:

> *Men and women have always sought by one means and another, to be together rather than apart. At first they were together by the simple expedient of being unicellular, and there was no conflict. Later the cell separated, or began living apart, for reasons which are not clear even today, although there is considerable talk. Almost immediately the two halves of the original cell began experiencing a desire to unite, again—usually with a half of some other cell. This urge has survived down to our time. Its commonest manifestations are marriage, divorce, neuroses, and, a little less frequently, gun-fire.*

Well, Wanda and my tears were streaming, but rather than paralyzed, we were near hysterical, mostly at the sketches. Once, Marsh came out, a confused smile on his face, asking if something was wrong, and for some reason we both screamed and our laughter sent him scurrying back to bed, no less confused.

As it got late and we wound down, I realized that, at least for me, this was one of those moments that you live for. I wondered if Ed would get a kick out of Thurber…and I found myself wondering if I, selfishly, hoped he wouldn't. I didn't want Wanda to share Thurber with anyone else.

Wanda and I had not done any hugging, except that once at the Deasels', but tonight it happened naturally…and I realized that with an affectionate hug like that, sex is not only not necessary but not even part of the equation. Again, like hugging your grandchild. Cool.

It was cold and blustery for Marsh's 4th birthday. My family all caravanned over to the Deasels' again. Eddie and Tad and their two boys made it this time, too. So, with Chris and Lizzy's four kids—their two oldest Jake and Samara who had been away at college for Marsh's last one made a point of making this one. Mac and Hiball's three, Abby and Abe's two, and now Eddie and Tad's two, and Allegra and myself, of course, we had quite the contingency. Naturally, Rose and Billy were there, and it turned out Marsh had invited Latree, a neighborhood friend.

In place of the fire engine, this time the Deasels brought in one of those huge enclosed bouncy thing-a-ma-jigs. Bounce houses I think they're called. My older grandkids are all very good at taking care of their younger cousins—not so much their younger siblings, though. Maci had taken the first turn caring for Randi, who was only two and would need some attention with everyone bouncing around. Some of the more anxious parents—especially Abby and Abe worried about Randi, and Sadie only being three and a half—peeked in through the little plastic window to ensure no broken bones, or deaths, were eminent. After watching for a while, they relaxed. You could see somewhat in through the plastic sides, too. Sadie was being well-taken care of. Edie and Tad's Berti was just one year older than Marsh and they seemed to hit it off right away.

Once again, all my kids were having a grand time with the Deasels. Even with the laughing and screams of the kids muffled in the bouncy thing, once again you could hardly hear yourself think. It was quite hilarious. I'm only five eight, and my wife, Louise, had been quite short, so my own children favored the side of brevity. The size differential was startling. Probably why it was so loud: only Jake, of the Arnetz's clan, and Hiball, both at a relatively meager six feet, were over five eight. My three daughters closer to five feet. So, we were yelling up and the Deasels down. I noticed Rose and my daughter Allegra again retreated to the shelter of the corner away from the bouncing, continuing their little alliance against bedlam.

At one point, both Sadie, five, and Berti had to be removed from the Bounce House. Both had been crying but wouldn't say why. When they had been retrieved, the older cousins had acted almost guilty, although I knew nobody would have intentionally done anything to sweet little Sadie, and Berti's older brother, Levi, may have 'accidentally' bounced into him…but nobody else would make him cry. Besides, he was a tough little bugger and, stouter than his older brother, he usually retaliated quite efficiently .

Suddenly, Jax, one of Chris and Lizzie's twins, stuck his head out the door and yelled: "Somebody better get in here, quick!" To his credit, Ed, who had been standing a little off from the mayhem and close to the bouncy, immediately stuck his head in through the doorway and yelled: "Marshawn! Stop! What the hell is wrong with you?"

We all tried to crowd around the entrance and could now hear high-pitched, not-having-fun screams emanating out and bouncing around, inside.

Ed yelled: "Marshawn, stop that! Now!" But the screams continued, along with a rather impressive barrage of swear words, including the big "F" one.

We were all trying to see what was happening through the cloudy, scratched-up plastic. From what I could see, it surprisingly looked like Marsh was kneeling over someone and flailing at him or her with his fists.

I could see Maci, Jax's twin sister, grabbed Marsh and pulled him off, as it turned out, of his friend, Latree. She handed a still swinging Marshawn to Ed, who in turn gave him up to his mother. Wanda hugged him to her, hard, to calm him down. Marsh was crying silently, his entire body heaving, unable to calm his breathing.

Latree came flying out of the bouncy, rather remarkable words bouncing out of his mouth. His nose and maybe other parts were bleeding. He ran straight into the office and out the door. I assumed heading home. My grandkids followed out the door of the bouncy, all grimacing guiltily.

Wanda was still holding Marsh tightly. Ed, who had had the front row viewing of the event, was still angry at Marsh, asking firmly: "Why did you do that?"

Samara, Maci, and Mac, and Hiball's oldest, Hadley, immediately came to Marsh's defense. Hadley saying angrily, "It's not Marsh's fault. That little shit was purposely knocking Sadie over and then picked a fight with Berti—again! We started to tell him to 'cool' it." (I'm guessing the word would have been: 'chill.') "When he called me a bitch and started cussing at us all, Marsh had had enough. It was cool. At first, he just went up to that little shithead and told him he had to go home. But the kid gave Marsh a shove. Marsh fell over backward on his butt and bounced right back up. It was really cool. He wrapped his arms around the kid, and they fell, Marsh on top. The kid started swinging at Marsh, yelling words *I've* never heard. Maybe I couldn't understand them. Anyway, Marsh was trying to block the kid's fists…we all were sort of frozen, not knowing what to do. Finally, Marsh popped him a good one—right on his noggin. The kid spit in Marsh's face and Marsh went medieval on him. Finally, Maci pulled him off and, well…you saw the rest."

Marsh's little body was still heaving. He wasn't crying out loud but was obviously really upset. He had his arms around Wanda who was still holding him, trying to calm him by rubbing his back.

No one knew what to say or do. I looked up at Lee and the other Deasels. They were all smiling…well I guess you'd say sporting shit-eating grins. Ed still looked angry. My kids and grandkids were all kinda shrugging and looking at each other with shit-eating grins on their faces as well. Squabbles happened occasionally between brothers and sisters and the cousins, but I couldn't remember ever seeing blood.

Ed tried to take Marsh, but Wanda turned away and walked over to a table and sat Marsh down on it. Marsh's face had been buried in Wanda's shoulder and he didn't want to let go. But he did seem to be gradually calming down, and as he finally let go of his mother, although he hadn't been crying out loud, you could see big tears had stained his chubby cheeks.

I walked over, bent, and looked him in the eye. I smiled and thanked him for protecting my grandchildren. He put his arms out and I picked him up and gave him a squeeze. It felt good at the time, but it turned out to be a big mistake.

Ed tried to take Marsh from me, but when I went to hand Marsh over, he lurched back and threw his arms back around my neck. Although it made me feel great to be hugging Marsh, I wasn't dumb enough to not realize Ed wouldn't be taking this rejection by Marsh joyously. I tried to sort of pull Ed into a three-way hug, but no cigar. He huffed away and told Wanda to pack up, that they had better get Marsh home.

I whispered to Marsh that maybe he should let Ed hold him. Marsh said nothing but I could feel his head shaking vigorously and he heaved a huge sigh. I was feeling such a conflicting sense of emotions: contentment and dread prevalent. Dread not only out of fear for how Ed would handle Marsh's rebuff, but Marsh was going to have to deal with what Latree was going to spread around the neighborhood. Marsh, according to Wanda, had already experienced—*watching* only, until now, we thought—fighting both within the neighborhood and between neighborhoods. But here Marsh would be facing big trouble. He had taken the side of White kids. Latree would probably see this as turncoat, treason. Marsh, due to…well me, I suppose, and his daycare and the Thursday group…was comfortable around—well, diversity I guess you'd say. I honestly didn't think he thought of color. Just injustice. Latree, I'm guessing, was not, unfortunately for us today, comfortable with diversity. Not his fault, of course. Nor would most of the kids in the neighborhood be comfortable with diversity. It was a Black neighborhood. The problem, of course, segregation presented. Yet this was Marsh's neighborhood. He needed to get along with these neighborhood friends. Despite my dread, I held onto him.

Wanda came over to take Marsh from me. Although she wouldn't look at me, I can only describe what I saw in her eyes as gloom. As she held Marsh, he looked at me sadly and said, "Latree is going to be mad at me."

Latree wasn't the only one mad, unfortunately.

CHAPTER 10

I was walking around Lake of the Isles with the lights from the Minneapolis skyline hazy through the falling snow in the early dusk. I had gotten several calls. I don't usually answer my phone when I'm enjoying myself, like today, out for this winter walk. There was a call I was fearing. Something told me I would be hearing from the director of the advocate program, so I was in no hurry to check my messages. Of course, it could be one of my kids. It could be urgent. But, I rationalized, the odds were it wasn't urgent. Nothing wrong with playing the odds. But, one of the grands could be sick, even dying, run over by a bus. Damn, why did I always have to be Norwegian? So, I took a deep breath and sneaked a peak. Naturally nothing urgent and, of course, one of the calls was from the director. I didn't like seeing that number. I doubt she was going to compliment me on reading *Is Sex Necessary* with my client. Since none of the messages needed immediate attention, I decided to continue my walk around the lake and return the calls later, at home, sitting down, with a strong drink in my grasp…especially for the call to the director.

I ended up not enjoying the rest of the walk. Every step in the compacted snow pounded out "dread, dread, dread." Each step. For an entire frickin half mile.

When I got home, I answered the other messages first. Drawing out the calls. You know, hoping maybe it'd get too late, and the director'd already have gone home, left the office, gone to bed. And, you know, she could, possibly, die ... peacefully of course, in her sleep.

When it was time for the last call, I threw down a shot of Tequila and followed up with half a beer in one long gulp. Never done that before. I sat there for a minute, my eyes watering, belched several times, thought I might throw up. Finally picked up the phone and my heartbeat started in. I could hear it, 'dread, dread—dread, dread.' I called.

She hadn't gone to bed. And when I told her it was me, I could tell by the way she said "Oh, Ryan" that it wasn't good news.

I started walking daily around the string of city lakes—Lake of the Isles, then Calhoun, now known as Bde Maka Ska. Then added Harriett. Then, one particularly irritable day, all the way to Nokomis and back. That's, like, a million miles. If there's snow, they sweep the blacktop paved trails around the lakes, and when the sun shines, they dry...unless they start to melt, refreeze, and become black ice. Which is treacherous. But no matter, around and around these lakes I went. It was late March and the air was warming. Lakes can be so soothing, so distracting, so transforming. On the occasional colder windy days, my face would feel like it was transforming into frost. Felt good, thou. The expanse of a lake gives the wind a good run at you. But it felt good to be cold. Like I needed to suffer. Maybe the wind would blow my melancholy away, freeze my fears.

I started showing up almost every evening at one of my kids' houses to see the grandkids. Until I got accused by the lot of them (they must talk?) that I just wanted a free dinner. True. Why not? Why eat alone? Why not kill three birds with one stone? Of course, Allegra would make me take her out to eat. Which was cool because we'd often also invite Rose. Which was bittersweet. I loved Rose. But she reminded me of Wanda and Marsh, and although I knew she knew something, she wasn't going to tell me, and I couldn't ask.

Ed, you see, had petitioned to be Marsh's advocate—the *only* advocate. The director had agreed, and it did make sense that Ed be *an* advocate. Why not have two? He hadn't been any knight in shining armor before, showing up infrequently at the Thursday gatherings. I wondered about now. It made sense to have two in case Ed doesn't show up. I mean, if Wanda and Ed were going to make a go of it, I didn't want to obstruct. But Ed, for whatever reason, had not proved to be a reliable advocate. Right? But, the big whallup, not that no longer acting as Marsh's advocate wasn't a whale of a whallup already, I was told I couldn't see Marshawn, at all, for a year.

"What!!" I had pretty much screamed into the phone when the director had told me this.

I heard a litany of reasons. But primarily: my presence would get in the way of Marsh bonding with Ed. Shit! What's worse than wanting something desperately but understanding why you can't have it? I couldn't even fault Ed...*if* he was serious about being a husband and father. I worried more about Wanda. What if it didn't work out with Ed? Marsh, just being a dumb kid, would recover. Not good—but kids are resilient. Not so much single mothers. They invest more emotionally in the relationship.

So, do I hope it doesn't work out with Ed? Then I could step back in and watch Marsh grow. Ensure all is OK. He was such a good kid. How could I just wipe him off my life? He was indelible. So was Wanda.

Like a spoiled kid, I immaturely (and selfishly I suppose) had argued with the director. "It's a free country!" That was pathetic, even if true. "Why can't I just go Wanda's and visit? And, I've made good friends at the Thursday 'gatherings.' There's no reason I can't visit there. It's just not fair!" I had realized I was embarrassing myself. But really, what about Ona even? I wanted to see her. I would miss her. Heck, I'd miss everybody. It wasn't fair!

The director had patiently reminded me that all of this was covered in our training and orientation. *"We are there for them. They not for us."* It was difficult, but I knew that was how it had to be. Marsh was not my great-grandchild. Wanda was not my granddaughter. And I needed to be OK with that.

So, I walked and walked and rode and rode my bike when winter eased into spring. I rode all over the place—and started doing more with all my grandkids. Of course, they made me think of Marshawn. Something became obvious to me: kids, when they're little, are all the same. They're just kids. Then life happens. My grandkids were being raised in privileged families. Was this wrong? I mean my children were all smart, attractive people with good jobs— should they feel guilty that they were able to send their kids to exceptional schools, give them 'good' educations? Enroll them in clubs and sports programs? Were they supposed to make themselves ugly? Their kids were certainly indulged…but they weren't spoiled. They didn't 'act' privileged. They were nice, polite, respectful, kind kids. So was Marsh—right now. He seemed just like my family. He deserved the same good education as my grands.

But what was life going to do to him, now? If he didn't continue in the advocacy program and ended up on the streets with Latrell, would he regress? Think life was not fair? Remember the Christmas with us and feel bitter? What would life teach him then? I tried to talk this over with Rose, but she was suspicious I was just digging for information she wasn't going to share with me. I wasn't angry with her. I understood…sort of. I was going crazy, knowing what had been and imagining what might happen if Ed didn't fulfill his obligation as an advocate and Wanda and Marsh were removed from the program. I tried to tell myself that Rose, Ona, or even Lee would alert me if things fell apart. I mean, what if Marsh started to resent me and even my grandkids?

My grands played soccer, had swimming lessons, were in the band, track, and Nordic and downhill skiing. Hadley in lacrosse. Chris and Lizzie's two oldest in Ultimate Frisbee! Man, the world had changed for 'exceptional' children. It was even tough for them to find time for Grandpa. Was this bad? I started going to all their 'events.' Buried myself in their lives.

I mean, I enjoyed it. But something was missing. I guess it was that although I loved them and they loved me, they didn't actually 'need' me. It was nice for them to have a grandpa, but they each had two grandpas already, and they would be fine without one of us. This rationalization did not, of course, make me feel any better. Then one day I found myself at a soccer practice—a practice! I told myself I needed to do something, again. Like get a life! Really *do* something. Like I thought I had been.

Should I become an advocate for another child? Why not? Maybe a White middle-class single mother? A kid more in in my wheelhouse? A culture I understood.

So, I mulled it over for a couple days. Bounced it off my kids: "Sure Dad. Good. But what about Marsh? You really going to just forget about him? How can you?" Bounced it off some friends: "Sure. Cool. Thought you were into that little Black kid?" Shit!

I decided to call the director. I asked her what she thought about me advocating for a White kid. Maybe a middle-class single parent? She answered that, yes, there was definitely a need for advocates in middle- and even upper-class families, but very few would stoop to admitting it. Just sweep the kid's problems under the Oriental rug. What would the neighbors think? More and more, a lot of the kids of better-off parents were into drugs or having mental health issues. That one threw me. When I was a kid, I never knew one kid that I was aware had mental health issues.

Mental health issues with young kids!? I mean, when I was a kid, some kids were weird and, like, ate their buggers or whatever. But 'mental health' issues?' That was for older people that life had somehow screwed up. Kids are just kids. Aren't they? They haven't had time to get screwed up. Well, the White middle- and upper-class kids, anyway. They had every advantage in the world, not like the kids in Marsh's or similar neighborhoods who grew up behind the eight ball and couldn't even see the pocket, much not owning it.

A thought popped into my mind, and I asked if there was, as I had wondered before, any plan to incorporate kids from the burbs with the city kids, like in an advocate program. You can guess what I was thinking. She told me some wealthy districts had a variety of programs and activities for pre-school kids. But that parents of kids in suburban schools felt their schools and teachers were superior to those in the city. There was no way they wanted to dilute or diminish their excellence by admitting to needing something like an advocate. And I was going: wait a minute! That's bullshit.

But, she said, coincidentally, they were looking at incorporating the latch-key program with the advocate program in the city.

"Latch key?" I had asked.

She told me that more and more there were two-career families and single, career-oriented parents that needed schools to take care of before-school and after-school needs for their kids.

Apparently, this already existed somewhat in the inner city and was gaining support in the burbs, but funding for this was always up in the air. Public funding (money) was always an issue in education, anywhere. It would be great if both programs were universal, but neither the advocate nor latch key had gotten much widespread traction, yet.

If the government saw education more as a priority, especially if incorporating volunteerism to reduce costs, the two programs could, and should, be instituted and consolidated everywhere.

I liked what she was saying. Regarding volunteerism, I've found most people, when given the opportunity to help other people, get great personal satisfaction from it. Why doesn't everyone realize you're happier making somebody else happy rather than selfish, shallow self-aggrandizement. Personally, I believe volunteerism is a total win-win deal. No? And volunteering to help a kid succeed, no matter where he or she lived or came from? C'mon. What would be more fulfilling?

"So, these would be older kids, like elementary school age, in the latch-key program?" I asked. "Is there anything available in the burbs for an advocate, somebody like me?"

"Let's not get ahead of ourselves. You're... Oh, wait," she suddenly spouted. "You know, I know of a woman, a friend of a friend, recently divorced with one kid, a boy, ten years old. Dad's now out of the picture—job overseas. I think they're getting divorced. She's fit to be tied." I've heard that cliched little phrase before, maybe even used it, but where it came from I had no idea, now that I thought about it. It seemed almost inappropriate the way the director used it. And if the mother is "fit to be tied," her kid is probably fit to be tied up.

"Her son, Kyle I think is his name, is having a difficult time. She, Kay, just started a job as an assistant analyst for an investment banking group. She's smart but has been out of the job market for a while. They apparently expect low pay to start and long hours, proving herself or something. She feels she's losing control. I pulled some strings and got her into a school with a latch-key program in the city, the Loring area, by where Kay works, just until the end of the school year. There's nothing in the local school district where they live."

There was a pause. "Yes?" I prompted.

"Well," she continued. "Kyle doesn't fit in. He might be the only rich White kid in the program."

"Might be good for him," I said.

"Well, yeah, maybe. That's why you might really be an asset."

I wasn't feeling especially excited about this. "Sounds like a 'Big Brother' kinda deal," I said.

"Well." She cleared her throat. "He was in that program during the divorce. I arranged that, too."

"What happened?" I asked.

"It just didn't work out. The kid is a handful. Needs somebody more like you."

"Like me?" I said, surprised. "I have no experience with problem kids."

"Look what you did with Marshawn. Look, I'm sorry about what happened there, but I'm aware how good a job you did."

"Look," I said, my ire roused thinking of Wanda and Marshawn. "First, Marsh was not a handful...or a problem kid."

"That's not what I hear," she interrupted.

"What? What do you mean?"

"Wanda's having a hard time with him. I get regular reports you know. Part of the program."

"What...what do you mean? Where's your new advocate? Where's..." I couldn't even spit out his name.

"Never mind. They're dealing with it, I guess. My point is you did a good job. This kid, Kyle, needs help. Why don't I set up a time for you, Kay, and Kyle to meet? Nothing official, for now. Just meet them. See what you think."

What I *was* thinking was *What the hell is going on with Marsh?* But, I said "Ok." I called. Kay sounded wired. Talked too fast but seemed relieved I agreed to meet. The house was in Minnetrista, a well-off, up-and-coming suburb neighboring Lake Minnetonka. When I pulled up to the bland modern monstrosity, my first thought was: *All this house for two people?* My sensibilities led me to disdain the concept that 'large' equates to 'good.' To me it was a waste of space: a large, pretentious box with windows.

Ok, relax, I told myself. *No judgments. I'm sure she's a nice person; she and her kid going through a hard time.* I, fortunately with my family, had had no experience with problem children, or, at least, children with this kind of problem. I wasn't sure I liked the feel of this whole deal.

When I reached the front door, I pushed the doorbell. Suddenly a shrill voice emanated from seemingly nowhere: "Yes?" I jumped and looked behind me. Again, less shrill, more impatient: "Yeess?" Embarrassed, I realized it was an intercom, and I hoped she couldn't see me turning in confusion. I stood on my tiptoes and, I'm afraid, yelled into the intercom, or in this case, outer-com, "It's me. Ryan Arnetz."

"Jesus!" I heard exclaimed. Then, quietly: "It's open. Come in."

I walked into a two-story foyer. White walls down and white carpeted stairs up with more white walls. But nobody in sight. I almost yelled out "Hello!" but figured she did grasp that I was here. I heard a voice speaking rapidly, gradually getting louder as it got nearer. Around a corner she came, a phone stuck to her ear. "Just a second," she said to the phone. Then: "Mr. Arnetz, could you come into the kitchen and have a chair? I must finish this call." I noticed she was dressed attractively, if a bit austere.

I followed her into a kitchen that would make mine look like it should have a wood-burning cook stove and ice box. The countertops gleamed polished silver and the walls and cabinets, here too, were white. I'd prefer my homey, grubby little kitchen with the ice box. "Please have a seat," she instructed. "I'll be done in a moment." I wanted to ask her where Kyle was, but her voice trailed away around a corner and dissipated into the white.

To make a long story short, Kyle ended up being in the 'theater' room, playing a game on a movie-theater size screen, with remarkably loud explosions careening off the walls…surround sound, I guess. It was overwhelming: things and people or avatars, I expect, were being blown to slivereens. When Kay finally convinced Kyle to exit the game, we trooped back to the kitchen, Kyle looking glum, Kay frazzled, me wanting to run.

Kay sat us at the table, me facing Kyle. Before we could say anything, Kay's phone rang. "Sorry," she said. "Work, again." Leaving Kyle and me facing each other. He pulled out his what must be a really smart phone—some kind of 'tablet' I suppose—and went back to his game. After a few minutes, I asked if he could put his apparatus down so we could talk. He looked casually up at me and informed me that I was not his dad.

So that's how it went. Kay was no help. I told myself after I left that I would just have to be patient. When Kyle realized I was simply trying to help him, he would understand eventually, as I hoped I would. Understand and trust me. The only thing I could initially see that was 'in my wheelhouse' was that we were both Caucasian. What else did we have in common? What would we do together? It wouldn't be playing video games. My nerves certainly couldn't handle those explosions. I could tell from his whitish pallor, his soft chubby little body, that he wasn't an outdoors kid or into sports. Oh, well. Kay needed help. Kyle needed something. I'd call the director tomorrow and tell her I'd give it a shot.

So, now the suddenly unctuous director was all for it. Fell all over herself thanking me. I wish I felt as good about it as she appeared to. But I couldn't shake the feeling that I was a traitor. Abandoning Marsh and Wanda. What if it didn't work out with

Ed? Something was sure up. I just couldn't picture Marsh being difficult. Maybe to Ed, but not his mother. Something wasn't right. How could I live with them finding some other advocate than me if Ed did leave? Or even, if I got through to Kyle baby, how could I just drop him? And Kay felt like a candidate for a breakdown. Yet one thing Marsh had said to me seriously bothered me: "Latree is going to be mad at me." Marsh had to exist in the world of his neighborhood…at least for now. Heaven forbid—maybe forever. Maybe Ed could get them out of that violent, poverty-stricken neighborhood? For the first time in my life, I fully realized the effects on a child growing up in poverty. It just wasn't fair. I didn't want to think about this. Maybe I should just join a club. A book club, a bridge club, a cribbage club, join the Scandinavian Foreign Legion…whatever. Forget about Marsh. Forget about Kyle.

But I couldn't.

I hadn't been able to get together with Kyle. Kay told me he had gotten kicked out of the latch-key program. I had no idea what had precipitated this. Kay had now placed him in a facility. No matter what euphemism, it was a mental health facility. I called the director and she told me this was temporary for the summer. When school started in the fall, they'd hopefully have found the right program for him. That Kyle would need somebody like me.

I almost felt guilty, but…I hate guilt. Anything that causes guilt should be cast out, avoided at all costs. It looked like there could be a big cost in this one.

But as spring rolled into summer, what really started to bother me was that Marsh would be starting kindergarten in the fall. Was he going to be ready? I had been sure of it. I hoped Ed would continue the progress. It was driving me nuts—what the director had said about Marsh being a problem. And in his class would be Latree and his neighborhood chums. How would Marsh adapt his wider life view he's gotten from his daycare—and Thursday-night gatherings—to the narrower neighborhood view?

There were a couple kids in the daycare that would be in his class. One was Ona's daughter, Remmi. Remmi was very shy and captivated us all in daycare with her mother's remarkable smile. Although taller than the other kids, she was quite delicate and appeared to be vulnerable. Marsh and Remmi got along well, and Marsh was often her protector. Although nothing too serious ever occurred in the group, she was occasionally picked on. Marsh always stepped up. But what would happen if Latree or a neighborhood boy, or maybe more likely, a neighborhood girl, picked on Remmi?

Another in his class would be Jay White Cloud's son, Arnie. Arnie was painfully passive. He seemed wary with almost everyone except Marsh. He was always pleasant, but the only time I saw him smile was when he was interacting with Marsh…a good sign of Marsh's character, I had thought. His dad, Jay, was massive, and Arnie, the only one taller than Remmi, was wide as Marsh was tall. A big kid. Arnie and Marsh had become friends. Being a Native American, how would he fit in with Latree and Marsh's neighborhood kids? I hoped his size would deter any bullying, but as soon as they found out how gentle he was, would he become a target? And how would all this be coming down for Marsh in school, caught in the middle? I'd never felt so helpless in my life. To not be able to do something that absolutely should be done is hell.

I wasn't aware of how Marsh was getting along in the neighborhood. Did he and Latree patch things up? What kind of kids was Marsh hanging around with? Could this be the cause of these so-called problems—the neighborhood? What would happen when school started? How would Marsh handle the potential clash of a Native American and his Black neighborhood friends? Wanda's neighborhood wasn't a ghetto, per se, but it was predominately Black and most definitely low income—poverty stained. Arnie came from the Indian community, just as poverty ridden, if not more so. Both neighborhoods had their gangs, of course. And crime was prevalent in both. How was Marsh handling this? How would he accommodate the clash of those two cultures, as well as his friendship with an Irish White boy and White Jewish girl? Marsh needed to be prepared for what to expect and how to mediate these culture clashes.

And Remmi? Ona rented a home in a neighborhood closer to the University of Minnesota. Although the homes were generally better maintained and there was less crime and violence, it was still low income…and in the same school district.

Some of the people in Ona's neighborhood were newly arrived in the US. Many spoke poor English—some none. Although Remmi was soft-spoken and very articulate, these were her neighborhood friends. For protection, of course, new gangs were forming in their neighborhoods, especially with the Somalis, I was told. Yet I was sure, with our yellow-haired president fostering ethnic and other divisions, and some 'leaders,' predominantly Republican, in the Senate promoting this divisiveness, every ethnicity would seek to band together for support and protection—thus gangs. I would think the most at risk now with the immigrant issue would be Muslims. This really concerned me because, although Ona and Remmi were Christian having come from the southeastern part of Nigeria which was, Ona had told me, peaceful, most in Remmi's neighborhood were Muslims…here, ironically, to escape violence apparently more prevalent in the northern part of Nigeria, but spreading. It wouldn't matter that Ona and Remmi weren't Muslims; they would feel the brunt of hatred for being something they weren't. School being another world, almost another planet, from our daycare group.

The gang aspect seemed like such a difficult one. They existed for protection and a need to 'belong,' yet really aggravated the divide. Even Black neighborhoods were divided by ethnicity and religion. I'm sure Remmi would, by association, be regarded as Muslim, as if that should make a difference, and although the mildest, least extreme child in our group, she would probably be reproached as a terrorist…an extremist. How ironic! And unfair.

It was driving me nuts. I wanted to be there to help Marsh sort all this out when he got to school. Would he remain friends with Remmi and Arnie? Had it been a mistake for him to have grown to school age in the unreal, tolerant, compassionate culture of his daycare and Thursday group? Was Latree jealous or whatever he was feeling with Marsh because of his closeness with my White grandkids? If they had been Black, but upper middle class, would that have made a difference? Or would even the economic disparity be too divisive? Why couldn't all of Marsh's neighborhood buddies be in our program or one like it? The more I thought about this, the more nuts I got.

CHAPTER 11

Whenever I went out to eat or whatever with Allegra and Rose, I always, with difficulty, resisted asking Rose if she was still in contact with Wanda. First, I knew, whether Rose wanted her to or not, Allegra would jump on me and defend Rose's right to privacy and tell me it was none of my business. But to me, it was my business. I decided I had to know about Marsh, and I had to start somewhere. Rose...

Once again, I sent her a text, asking her to call me. It was a Friday afternoon, so I wasn't sure when she'd have time to look at it, but within two minutes, she called.

"Hey, Ryan. Long time no see. What's up?"

"What are you doing tonight?" I asked.

"Tonight? Why? Are you and Allegra going out?"

"Nope. Can I buy you a drink? Even dinner if you're up for it?"

"This a date? Or do you just want some information? If I tell you I won't talk about Wanda and Marsh, still want to take me out?"

"It's not a date," I said, buying time for a comeback. "I love you. I just want to see you."

"Poppycock! I realize it's hard not to love me, since I'm so gorgeous and funny and 'young!' and all. But you're as transparent as a cellophane bag of bullshite."

I laughed. Rose rarely talked like this. I think she was attempting to be firm. "Besides young, you're too smart, as well as too beautiful to date a boring old fart like me." Pity, although admittedly smarmy, sometimes works. Yet, I was also right. She was too smart and beautiful…and young…for an antiquated quinquagenarian.

She laughed. "You need to work on your come-on lines, old man. Pity is beneath you."

I agreed and was, even if desperate, embarrassed.

"Look, I love you, too," she said. "I'm tied up [there's that tempting phrase, again] all weekend. I'd be glad to have you buy me dinner any time…but I absolutely can't and won't share confidences from Wanda with you. Sorry. I know how hard it is for you. I'm sure you're going crazy. Why don't you try Lee?"

"Lee?" I said, surprised. "Wouldn't she be less likely to talk to me than you?"

"No, fool. Wanda talks to me in confidence. So, I can't betray that. But Lee…she just knows what's going on. You know her. If she think's it'd be good for Marsh or Wanda to see or talk to you, she'll arrange it. And I'll tell you this much: Talk to her, soon!"

"What?!" I exclaimed. "What's wrong?"

I heard her say something to someone. "Look. I gotta go. Talk to Lee. I'll see you next week if you like. I gotta go. By, hon." I assumed the 'hon' implied sympathy and regret.

Of course, I understood. Rose wouldn't be Rose if she betrayed her promise to Wanda not to snitch. Lee, huh? I didn't have a number for her, so I called the garage. Albert, the youngest

Deasel, answered. And, yes, as I believe I've told you, he was known as Fat Albert. He was, indeed, massive, the largest and roundest of the Deasels. He gave me Lee's cell number without hesitation. When I called it, she answered:

"Hey, Ryan. How they hangin'?" Lee was always so swank, much the opposite of Rose.

"Haven't paid much attention lately. Low I guess." Lame, lamentably inadequate response, I knew. But I had no idea what would be funny and inoffensive to her…and, besides, it was true. I had been feeling highly inadequate lately. Not so much sexually—well yah, that too—but more just kinda lost—everything hanging rather low for sure. "You got time to talk?" I asked.

"I've been waiting for you to call, man. You must be dying over there."

"You've got no idea," I answered, sounding pitiful.

"Oh, I think I do. If you hadn't called me, I was going to call you."

My heart skipped a beat. "Is something wrong?"

"You might say that, Jack."

Jack? What the hell's that mean, I wondered. Like 'hit the road, Jack'?

"Hey," she said when I hadn't said anything for a beat. "What you doin' tonight?"

"Why? I mean, nothing."

"Can I buy you a drink?"

The old heart jumped. "Yeah, sure, you betcha."

I had to hold the phone away from my ear as a deafening roar bounced off a satellite and rattled my brain. "So, where do they serve lutefisk? You know I betcha. Yah?"

I laughed, loud for me, but meek compared to her. "You hungry?"

"Don't us Deasels always look hungry?"

"No. You look like you are always satiated."

Another roar deafened me. "Satiated! You can't use fancy words like that with a dumb broad."

"Yeah. You're about as dumb as a fox," I said, my cheeks getting sore from smiling.

"Well, I think you just called me fat, but I'll forgive you if *you* buy *me* something to eat. And I will tell you what's going on with Marsh and Wanda."

"Well, you're hardly fat." I had to save myself. "You're probably the most potent, sagacious 'broad' I ever met, though."

Another roar. "'Potent!?' Don't know what I think about that one. 'Sagacious' sounds a little sexy. You comin' on to me, boy?"

I swallowed hard. Was I? "You like Cuban?" I asked before I ran out of 'safe' euphemisms.

"Cuban? No shit? Yeah, sounds good."

"You know where Victor's is...on Grand?"

"The place that looks like a shack from the street...like a place a Black man might barbecue up some ribs?"

"Yup. That's the place. Food's great. We'd need to get there before dinner time, though. It isn't very spacious, and it gets crowded."

"Ok, my little Scandinavian Cuban. See you in twenty."

"Uh, thanks," I said.

"Why thank me? You're buying. See you, man."

I got there in fifteen. It's not far from where I live. Frequently there's a line out the door, but I didn't see one. I hurried in and luckily got the last table. The place, besides being small, was popular. I, and obviously a lot of other folks, loved that it looked like a ragged shack on the outside. On the inside, you felt like you'd strolled into Cuba.

Lee got there in about thirty. I was already on my second beer, and since I wasn't much of a drinker, I could feel them. Although

Victor's patrons were used to an ethnically diverse patronage, everyone looked at the six-foot-plus Black woman—now with bright orange hair—who strode in like she owned the place and looked at everybody like she might kick them out onto the street if they didn't love her hair color.

I stood up to greet her; she bent, grabbed my ears, and planted a powerful smooch right on my lips, causing me to fall back into my chair, feeling like I'd received a rather invigorating jolt of electricity. She roared again at, I'm sure, the stunned surprise on my face. If someone hadn't seen her enter, they were now well aware, as I certainly was, of her presence. The tables were tight in Victor's, and the guy that would be sitting behind her chair doffed his tam, said excuse me, and moved to the chair on the other side of his table.

Lee smiled, said "Thank you," and held her fist up for a bump. The middle-aged dude looked at the fist, twice as big as his, and gave it more of a quick tap than a bump.

When she sat, she beamed at me. "Good to see you, Ryan. How's the family?"

"Good, good," I answered. "Thanks for seeing me."

She frowned. "Of course, bro." She actually called me 'bro.' I loved it.

We ate. I had one more beer, made it last through Lee's four. We talked for about two hours. The waiter gave us a dirty look once, I suppose because we were taking up a table for too long. When Lee asked him what his problem was (I saw where Wanda got her glare from), it looked like his problem was now filling his tight jeans.

It turned out Wanda was quite concerned about Marsh. He had become withdrawn. Wouldn't talk at all sometimes…shades of his mother. Latree had not forgiven him and had turned some of the kids in the neighborhood against him. Marsh got along great with several of the girls in the neighborhood, but that had only made it worse with several of Latree's gang…and it sounded like it was a gang. They had come up with a 'sign' that represented their neighborhood, and there were what sounded a lot like 'hazings' each member had to go through and do to the neighboring neighborhood kids. Nothing too serious yet, I guess. At least it appeared there had been no weapons so far. Most of the kids were about Marsh's age, from maybe four to six. Christ, do they really start that young?

A lot of the neighborhood activity happened in the evening or at night. Wanda had a 7:00 p.m. curfew for Marsh, but he was fighting this. Apparently, there had been retaliations from other neighborhoods and Marsh felt pressure to have his bros' backs. If he didn't show, he would lose face. Latree was especially hot on him, Lee said, using the birthday episode for kindling. He would tell the hood kids that Marsh didn't have their backs, constantly hassling him about having sided with the Whities against him.

Then one night Marsh had come home long after curfew, crying. Wanda, who was going to punish him for being late, relented, worried he had been hurt. Marsh did not cry easily. I guess Marsh and his 'gang' had infiltrated Arnie White Cloud's neighborhood and were going to give some Indians an ass-whooping. You'd think an ass-whooping at four or five couldn't be too serious, but older gang members, as in this situation, would come along occasionally. Kind of a gang boot camp, it seemed. Some of these older kids were known to have carried weapons. That could change the nature of a whoopin' considerably, Lee pointed out. *How is Marsh gonna handle this crap* was what I was thinking.

As it turned out, Arnie and a few of his buddies had confronted them, protecting their territory. Arnie, twice as big as any of Marsh's tribe, had surprisingly clomped a couple of them on the head and sent them all scampering.

But Latree, who had heard Marsh talk about his friend, Arnie, egged-on Marsh, who had hung back during the confrontation, to go back and fight Arnie. Marsh felt pressured and didn't want to lose face so had wandered back with Latree and some of the older guys egging him on. When Arnie saw Marsh, he hollered: "Hey, Marsh. What you guys think you're doing?" Marsh had run home, knowing what Latree and his pack would think.

"Damn!" was all I could say when Lee was done. "Where has Ed been during all this?" I asked.

Lee shifted in her chair and cleared her throat. "He's been around most of the time, especially Mondays, of course." She smiled and batted her eyes, almost guiltily. "I'd say he's worried about you showing up."

"Is he going to the Thursday gatherings?"

"He makes most...well, some of them," Lee answered. "Yeah, maybe just some of them I guess, but..."

"But...what?" I asked.

"Well." She hesitated. "Do you talk to any of the people from that group?"

I had to answer: "No. The director told me I couldn't." As soon as I said it I was embarrassed and pissed off. *Cripes, I should be able to talk to whomever I want to! Who does she think she is? Why am I such a wimp?* I suppose she could make it difficult for me, but I assumed there were people over her who might not be so inflexible. Too much power in small hands not a good thing.

"Hmm. You might want to rethink that," Lee said, looking at me like I was a wimp. "It seems to me Wanda mentioned you had the hots for a cool, good-looking Black lady there? You know, somebody like me, cool and good-lookin, only half my girth—although not so potent or, what was it—satiated?"

I smiled. "There's nothing wrong with your girth," I answered, having no idea how to banter with a Black woman, especially one that could beat the crap out of me, and more especially about her body.

She smiled, yes, mischievously, even coyly. "Oh? What's that mean?"

Ok, I was totally out of my element. I doubted Black and Scandinavian humor danced gracefully. "Well…" I stammered and couldn't help a glance down at her breasts. She had on a rather tight sweater. She suddenly sat up and pointed them at me. They demanded attention. I had been trying not to glance all meal. I suppose three beers did the trick. She didn't dress sexy at all, but she just was shapely and it showed. She couldn't hide it. She could star in a movie of Amazon women. She had caught me glancing and I could feel myself blushing.

She burst out in laughter loud enough Victor, himself, looked out the window from the kitchen. "I like you, Ryan. You're cute. But if you're going to get anywhere with this skinny lady, you'd better get some balls and brush up on your moves. You flirt about as well as…well, as well as a moose."

"A moose!" I said, loud enough for Victor to take another peek. I did as well. Then reminded myself she was gay.

She smiled, and I believe I detected a blush. "Well, I couldn't come up with anything that wouldn't shock your lily-white ass."

I tried to look offended.

"Anyway, talk to this pretty lady, will ya?" At the moment, again probably due to three beers, I had lost interest in the skinny lady.

"Really?" I answered lamely. "Why are you suggesting I talk to her, exactly?"

"Just talk to her. She'll be our spy. I'm guessing she's willing. Well, let's split this bill and hit the road, Jack. This Cuban shit wasn't so bad."

"No way!" I said, a little too loudly, again compromising any modest sensibilities but wanting to act like I had suddenly grown some kahunas. Although I had to admit, sitting there with this remarkable woman gave me courage, a sense of confidence I didn't know I had. I realized, although I rarely, or never, would talk loud or brash in a restaurant or anywhere out in public, I wasn't embarrassed or feeling 'compromised.' Bullshit. Why should I restrain myself just because it was a Scandinavian stereotype to be restrained? I was going to need this newly discovered aplomb, I figured, if I was going to regain being Marsh's advocate…and gain some respect from Lee. "I said I was paying. So I am," I asserted, as boldly as I could.

"Ok, ok," she said, laughing. "Better leave a decent tip."

Outside, before we separated, I tried again: "Why do you want me to call—Ona is her name?" This was going to bug me. Probably wouldn't be able to sleep. Guess I'd just have to call her tonight.

"Just call. Let her know what I said. See what she thinks."

"And what about Marsh and Wanda?" I felt I was left hanging. "And Ed…how is Marsh reacting to Ed?"

Lee paused. "Not good. He's, I guess you'd say, 'dismissive' toward Ed.'"

"What's that mean?" I asked.

Lee leaned down, went nose to nose with me. I didn't dare look her in the eye. I knew what was there. All I could watch was a finger tapping my chest like a jackhammer.

"You goin' call her." A command not a question. "Then we'll see what you're made of." A last firm tap, punctuating the sentence with a period, ended our little meeting.

So, before I thought about it and chickened out, when I got home, I dug out my list of kids, parents, and advocates and called Ona. It was driving me nuts why Lee would have, basically, ordered me to call Ona. And after what she told me about Marsh's current struggles, I wasn't going to be sleeping anyway until I knew why. I was surprised she had told me as much as she did. I assumed she must be quite concerned herself…and obviously expected me to do something about it. I was also very curious about what was going on between Wanda and Ed.

I was expecting to leave Ona a message, and when she answered right away, I was so shocked, I hung up. What an idiot! I felt like a nervous teenager. When I had heard her Bahamian lilt, I froze. I had no idea what I was going to say…and I *was* nervous. I had to go take a leak before I could call back.

Naturally, just after I got the flow going, my phone rang. I was still holding it (the phone) and it made me jump, spraying the floor. It was the number I had just called…so, Ona. I figured I had to answer, so I attempted to shut off the flow—something I was not very good at. It was becoming harder and harder to get it going these days…something I was not going to share with Ona. "Hello?" I tried but it came out more as a grunt.

"Ryan?" she said.

"Oh, hi Ona." I attempted, but I could tell I wasn't going to be able to talk and hold. Maybe ten years ago. And I'd talked to people, well men anyway, who had taken a leak while we were talking on the phone and you could totally hear the little waterfall. I could hardly do this with Ona. "Can I call you right back?" I asked.

"Didn't you just call me?" she said, sounding confused, or skeptical…probably of my sanity.

"Yes," I squeezed out, trying to hold the dribble. "I'll explain. I'll call you right back."

"Hmm… Ok," she said.

I hung up and, of course, once forcibly interrupted, the flow didn't want to resume. But I knew as soon as I quit trying, and called Ona, it would recapitulate. God, I had an ominous feeling about how this conversation would go.

Finally, after some deep breaths, I completed the task, flushed, sat on the toilet, and called her right back. Of course, she picked up right away and the water was still swirling down the drain. Embarrassed, I almost hung up again. But then what would I do? I wouldn't be able to call her back. She'd think I was nutso, and I realized I still wasn't sure what I was going to say.

She laughed when she answered. "What is going on, Ryan?"

I thought of lying and blaming it on my phone or something, but from experience, I knew lying only gets you in more trouble. "Uh…"

She saved me: "Where have you been? Haven't seen you for ages. Wanda mentioned something about you being vexed with the advocate thing?" I loved her voice. She had a slight, almost aristocratic accent. I could tell she was highly educated. Spoke slowly and distinctly.

"Yeah," I said, still buying time to think. "How'd you know it was me that had called?"

She giggled. "Ryan, you're going to need to graduate to the modern world. You obviously don't understand your smartphone. You're in my phone, so it tells me who is calling."

I had gotten a smartphone a while ago, but I knew little of its magic. I remembered her asking my number and doing something with her phone at one of the meetings. Of course, I had gotten all excited, assuming she needed my number to call me. No call was ever resurrected, however. At least I was in her phone, which I'm aware means nothing, but it still felt good.

"So, where have you been? What's the problem?""

"Well, um, yes," I stumbled. "Wanda's new fella petitioned to be the sole advocate for Marshawn."

"Oh? Why not both of you?"

Obviously, Wanda (and Ed) had been mum on this. "Well, yeah. That's what I had suggested. I mean it kinda was that way for a while. But Ed, her new guy, felt I would be getting in the way of his relationship with Marshawn."

"Hmm. Really? That's not copasetic."

"I agree," I said. "Great word by the way." I used it all the time.

"Oh?"

"Yeah, definitely."

"Definitely 'a great word,' or 'definitely' you agree you're inhibiting their relationship?"

This is really going well. I know she thinks I'm an idiot. "Uhh, both I guess. I'm trying to see it from Ed and Wanda's point of view. I've been told to stay away, irregardless." Shit! I hate people that say 'ir'-regardless. "Sorry," I said.

"Sorry for what?"

"Uhh…never mind." I am an idiot. "That's why I haven't been at the meetings."

"Well, Ed hasn't been at the meetings very often. I've noticed you with Marsh in the past. I think he respects you. I don't think he accepts Ed. He needs you, I'd say. He's been noticeably withdrawn. He's changed. I think Wanda's worried. He hasn't been as friendly as usual with Remmi, and last meeting, he and Arnie, Jay White Cloud's boy, almost got into a fight. And they had been such good friends."

"I think I know what's going on there," I said.

"Oh?"

"Do Ed and Wanda seem to be getting along?" I asked.

"Well…Ed and Asia…"

"She's still the teacher?" I interrupted.

"Yes. But the word is she may be leaving. But, anyway, Ed and she talk a lot. Ed really has her ear."

"They talking about Marsh?"

"We-e-ll... I'm not sure I should speak about this."

"How come?"

"We-e-ll... We are worried about Wanda. Wanda and I and a couple of the parents and advocates met your friend Rose and Wanda's cousin Lee after last Thursday's meeting and..."

After a very pregnant pause I said, "Yes, and?"

"Look, I'm going to tell you this because from what I could tell you were good for Wanda as well as Marshawn."

Another pause. I was on the edge of my toilet seat, going nuts. "Yes?" Then I plopped out with: "Ona. Would you meet me for a drink?"

After a very pregnant pause: "You mean a date?"

Of course I'd die for a date with lovely Ona. But I said, "No. I just want to talk about Marsh. How about a cup of coffee?"

"Oh, Ryan, I just shouldn't."

'Why!?' I managed not to scream.

When I didn't say anything more, she continued: "Jake and I are going through a rough patch."

"I thought you had broken up?"

"We-e-ll, he wants to make it work. So, we're trying. He's not feeling very secure at the moment, I don't believe."

Naturally he wants to make it work. He'd be a fool not to.

"So, I don't want to rattle the palms."

Cool, I thought: not 'rock the boat' but 'rattle the palms.' I wondered if that was a cliché where she came from. But not cool that Jake might see me as a threat. Great, here I am, an old, gray-haired, near-sighted, moderate, conventional, timid, undaring, boring Scandinavian and I'm a 'threat' to Ed and Jake. Should I be proud? No. Pride is a pretension not flowing in my blood...and ridiculous, besides. Me a threat? But I have to say I did feel a change. My world was expanding. I was finding being drawn out of my comfort zone was rather interesting.

"But I tell you what. Jake will not be there next Thursday. As a matter of fact, he's missed as many meetings as Ed. Why don't you come as a guest advocate for my daughter? She always enjoyed you."

"Really?" The suggestion got me off my uncomfortable toilet seat. "You think I could?"

"You'll be my guest."

"Maybe I should talk with the director?"

Ona laughed. "You really are conventional. Just come, Ryan."

I was excited. As excited as I get. "I'm going to say OK…for now. I may run it by the director, though."

She laughed again. "Whatever."

"Wait," I said. "What did you guys and Rose talk to Wanda about?"

Another long pause. I found I was holding my breath. "Several of us are wondering if Ed and Asia have something going on. I think so."

"Yikes. What does Rose say?"

"She's the one who set up the meeting. She comes occasionally as a surrogate for Ed. As you probably know, she's rather perceptive. She's worried about Wanda."

But Wanda must suspect something then, too, I thought. *And if Rose can be Ed's replacement why in the hell can't I?*

"As a matter of fact, Rose asked me about you. You must not see her much?"

"Why do you say that?"

"Well. She told me to say hi from her when I talked to you. Almost like she was encouraging me to call you. I supposed she assumed you wouldn't be calling me. I would have called you if it weren't for Jake. But I'm really pleased you called, Ryan."

Rose. Beautiful, wonderful Rose. She couldn't break Wanda's confidence, but she knew both Lee and Ona could clue me in. *Oh, I do love that woman. Such a good friend.*

"You want me to pick you up?" I asked.

"No," she answered. "But I'll tell you what, meet me in the parking lot and we can walk in together."

"Oh, great, Ona. Thank you so much. I'll call you if I change my mind."

"See you there. Bye, Ryan."

"Bye, hon." I hoped the 'hon' didn't offend her, but she, as well as Rose, is as sweet as they come. When I hung up, I realized how much I had changed. I mean, I was thinking I wanted to invite all four of these women—Ona, Rose, Lee, and Wanda—over for dinner. And it made me laugh what the neighbors would think. Heck, my kids would get a kick out of it, but what would my old conservative friends think? They would be uncomfortable, if not petrified, to be at that dinner table. Lee, alone, would scare the crap out of them. Before Wanda and Marshawn, who would have thought that my four favorite people in the world right now, aside from my family and old friends, were a collection of Black women?

Not me.

CHAPTER 12

So, Kyle had not gone away and neither had guilt. Kyle would be telling people who were trying to help him "you're not my dad" all summer long. I hated to feel like this, but he had done nothing to get me even a little interested in trying to help him. I had no idea how to help him. He certainly didn't want my help. Kay made me nervous as hell. It just seemed like a disaster already happening. I certainly didn't feel qualified to deal with either of them. I felt they *both* needed a mental health facility... at the least. But, come fall, I'd do what I could to help stabilize Kyle's life. I'd said I would. What's worse—guilt or inadequacy? They probably made good bedfellows. In the meantime...Marsh and Wanda.

I pulled into the parking lot early. I still hadn't decided if this was a good idea. How would Wanda react to seeing me there? How would Marsh react? Would he be mad at me? What if he was glad to see me and Ed was there? Also, a dread that I kept pushing out of my mind: how would the director react if, or more likely when, she found out? Would she buy that I was acting as a surrogate for Jake? I felt I could, almost, justify it because it was Ona's invitation. Of course, the director'd have Kyle baby as leverage to hold over me. I probably never should have agreed to help. Well, I can't really say that. I did ask for it.

Just as I was deciding I shouldn't be doing this, Ona pulled up next to me. It was late June, a nice night. The days were at their longest, so it was still light. I couldn't hide in the dark. Ona looked over and her face lit up. Remmi leaned forward and waved to me. Ok, not leaving.

We three walked in together, Remmi holding my hand. Asia was there and a few others. I couldn't help but notice that Asia did not look exactly happy. Was it me? Or was there more going on? Everyone else there came over and it was like old times. I had gotten to know these people well, and there wasn't an asshole in the group.

I felt a pressure behind me, turned to see Jay White Cloud's chest.

"Where you been, man? We need you here, you know?" His voice was deep and soft.

"Good to see you, Jay," I said, ducking a response, shaking a huge meat of a hand. Arnie walked by and gave me knucks.

As more people entered, I got hugs and handshakes. Asia kept her distance. Shot a few darts my way that hit the target. No Wanda, Marsh, or Ed, yet. When I turned to talk to Ona, she directed me with her eyes to the door. I knew what she meant, and I was afraid to look. "Is Ed with them?" I asked her.

She shook her head.

When I turned, I saw that Marsh had seen me. Although he managed to remain stoic, I saw tears welling up. God, I couldn't look at him. I wanted to run over and grab him and hug the crap out of him. When I looked up at Wanda, her face was passive. Neither of them moved. When I smiled, Wanda took Marsh's hand and walked him over to a table that Arnie was sitting at, both ignoring me. I was almost sorry I had come. My old heart was in a knot.

Ona put her hand gently on my shoulder. "Give them a minute, and then go talk to them," she whispered.

When I got home that night, I literally cried myself to sleep. I'm not known for being emotional. Much the opposite. It's hard for me to cry, but once I got going, I couldn't quit. My mind was just dark. I was trying not to think about anything. I just laid down on my bed sniveling until I fell asleep.

Wanda had ignored me all night. Never even looked at me that I saw. Was unusually distant from everyone all night. Marsh stayed at one end of the table with Arnie on the other. Shahlla and Heather were still the aids. Heather had coloring crayons spread out on the table. All the kids at the table were coloring quietly except Marsh. He was by himself at the end of the table. It was like all the kids understood that something was going on and gave him space. Could they really be that intuitive? That empathetic?

I had finally walked over to Marsh and sat next to him. He didn't look up. In front of him was a coloring book page with different races of people on it. He had colored all the faces black...except one. It was a guy in a suit and tie. He had taken a red crayon and was making an X across the face, over and over again.

I asked if I could give him a hug. He nodded slowly but didn't turn toward me. I put my arms around his shoulder and squeezed the best I could.

I asked him if he knew why I hadn't been around. He started making huge X's across the entire page. Not angrily, but intently.

Asia walked up to me and asked if she could talk to me. I kissed Marsh on his forehead. Said I missed him.

"Are you aware of how angry Ed is going to be?" she asked me, when we had escaped to a corner.

Anger welled up inside me. "Where is Ed? Marsh's advocate!"

"He had some work-related issues," she responded.

"Oh? How do you know this?" I asked.

She sputtered a bit. "None of your business," she finally spit out. "Does the director know you're here?"

"I'm here as Remmi's advocate. You noticed I walked in holding Remmi's hand? Ona invited me since Remmi's advocate was not here."

"Yeah, she told me. You think I'm stupid? You've usurped Ed's rights. You have no right being here."

"You're sounding like Ed's advocate. Is there something you'd like to tell me?"

Although she acted angry, it was fear I saw in her eyes.

"I think you should leave. Now!"

I felt almost evil, because I could tell Ona was right. So, I smiled, knowingly, and yes, malevolently. But come on, she deserved it. I said goodbye to Heather and the kids at the table, Marsh not looking up, and high-fived Arnie as I walked by. I went over to Remmi's table, gave her a little hug and said goodbye to Shahlla and the kids. Ona met me as I turned and gave me a huge hug. I thanked her and she gave me a kiss on my forehead. Kinda weird. "I'm glad you came Ryan. I think things will sort themselves out." She touched my cheek and gave me a sad, but I think she meant it as an encouraging, smile. Wanda was still ignoring me.

CHAPTER 13

S tarted biking every day. Round and round the city lakes once again. My mind was a mess, but I was getting my body in good shape. I had no idea what to do, so I kept my eyes on the trail, tried to keep my mind empty. The line from an Eagle's song—"Don't let the sound of your own wheels drive you crazy"-- got stuck in my brain. Started to drive me crazy. Like watching telephone poles whip by in the car, I tried to focus on the cracks in the pavement—slap by, slap by, slap by. Each day I'd pick a good line from a song and sing it to myself, over and over to the sound of my bike's wheels driving me.

A good thing: the director hadn't called reprimanding me for showing up at the Thursday gathering. So, Asia hadn't squealed, yet. Neither had Wanda said anything, apparently. So, cool there. But now what? I decided to call Rose and asked her if she might consider my outstanding offer of a dinner…and invite Wanda and Marsh along. Could that work? Would they consider it? My heart was heavy. Wanda had been sullen all that night. I didn't know if she was unhappy seeing me there, or upset about what I assumed she at least suspected about Ed and Asia. And poor Marsh. After I finished feeling sorry for myself after that night, I considered Marsh. He had certainly not been his gregarious self. He and Arnie had not even spoken. Of course, he apparently wasn't speaking to anyone. And I still found it remarkable that everyone had left him alone. I noticed several people's sideways glances toward Marsh, and I could feel eyes trailing me up until I left. So I know they were concerned. And Asa had spent the entire evening wandering around the room, not engaging anyone—or vice versa. Except me, of course. Did everyone suspect something was going on between Asia and Ed?

Rose said she'd love to have dinner…with or without Allegra. But no dinner with Wanda and Marsh and she would not talk about Wanda. When I responded that I respected her opinion and just needed advice, she referred me to Lee, again. I hung up, having agreed to dinner Friday with her and Allegra. "But I'm not paying then," I had childishly avowed before hanging up, not allowing Rose the opportunity to respond. Childish pouting, I know.

Just before I was going to call her back to apologize, Lee called. She told me Wanda had not told Ed I had come to the gathering, but Marsh had let it slip. Ed was going to call the director. Had I heard from him yet? "Her," I said. "No. But I will, I'm sure."

My sulk turned surly: "So, what's up with Ed? I could tell there was something going on with Asia…"

"How'd you know that?" Lee interrupted.

"I said something about her and Ed, and…and I saw it in her eyes."

"Saw what?"

"Fear I'd say."

"Fear?"

"Yeah. Like she was caught with her hand in the cookie jar."

"That's not the analogy I'd use," Lee said. "But I understand, I guess."

"What does Wanda think?"

"She doesn't," Lee answered and laughed.

"Doesn't what?"

"Think. About Ed and Asia."

"I thought women always knew?" I said.

"It takes a while to 'know,' you know? Look, Ed's not a bad guy. They get along pretty well. If there's a problem, it's more with Marsh. He doesn't mind being scolded by his mother—he's very sensitive with Wanda—but he rejects any discipline from Ed. He doesn't really relate to Ed."

"I assume they're intimate, Ed and Wanda?"

"Whatcha think, homey? Except she's let it slip the romance angle is fading."

"Isn't that suggestive of and a natural consequence of Ed's involvement with Asia?"

"Whoa. You're smarter than you look there Ryan baby."

I laughed. "Thanks, I guess. Look, could you, me, Wanda, and Marsh go out to eat…or do something?"

There was a pause. "I think it might be best to let this thing with Ed play out. I agree with you. But let's let Wanda figure it out. Seeing you is just going to muddy the waters. Sorry, baby."

What could I say? She was probably right. Of course, how would I stay sane in the meantime? As if prompted, my phone rang. Allegra had put all my significant people and numbers into my 'contacts.' So I knew it was the frickin', smarmy director. I almost didn't answer but realized I'd have to face at least a tongue-lashing eventually.

"Hello?" I answered as innocently as possible.

"Ryan," I could tell from the tone of her 'Ryan' it was going to be at the least a reprimand. "What were you thinking?"

"Hello, how are you doing?" Lame, I admit. "What do you mean?" I attempted to maintain my innocence charade.

"You know damn well what I mean! Why did you break our agreement and show up at last Thursday's meeting?"

I wanted to point out that it wasn't an 'agreement.' It was more an 'order.' Instead, I defended myself. "I was asked by Ona, Remmi's—"

"I know who Ona is," she interrupted.

"Ona asked me to come as Remmi's fill-in advocate. It seems Jake has not been as involved as she liked."

"You think I'm stupid, Ryan?"

"Ask her," I replied.

"You're insulting my intelligence, Ryan. We all know why you were there. You're jeopardizing your role as a future advocate in the program."

This scared me. I wanted to tell her about our suspicions about Ed and Asia but recognized that this was probably not a good idea…at least not right now. "I'm sorry," I tried. "I just know Wanda and Ed are going through a rough spell with Marshawn. As Marshawn and Wanda's *former* advocate, I was concerned."

"You're not making it any easier for Ed by buddying up to Marshawn and Wanda."

I started to say I hadn't even talked with Wanda, much less 'buddied-up.' but I knew that was lame. Settled for less confrontational, more Norwegian: "I'm sorry."

"I'm sorry, too, I'm afraid. I'm going to withdraw you from the program—"

"Wait!" I almost shouted. "I promise to turn Ona down next time she requests I advocate for Remmi—"

"Don't give me that bull, Ryan."

"Look," I was getting desperate, "what can I do? I promise I won't contact or see either Wanda or Marshawn, unless Ed drops out of the program."

"I'll tell you where you can redeem yourself." I knew where she was going with this. "You can visit Kyle and prove to be a good advocate for him." Blackmail.

"You mean when school starts in the fall?"

"No, now. He's not being responsive at all at the mental health facility." I wanted to argue that if mental health professionals couldn't deal with the poor kid, what could I do? But she had me by the you-know-whats. "If you're such a concerned advocate, see what you can do."

I sighed and resigned myself. "Alright. When?"

"I'll have Kay get ahold of you. Work out when you can visit Kyle, with her or without. If something good doesn't come of this, Kay'll end up in the mental health facility with her son."

Exactly, I thought. I had bad feelings about this. I really expected any time that the truth would come out about Ed and Asia, and then, of course, Wanda would not want Ed as Marsh's advocate. I certainly didn't want my availability to return jeopardized, which, of course, it already might have been. I rationalized that both Kay and Kyle were in dire need of some kind of help, and the director had me by the short hairs. So, I'd wait for Kay to call me, if she did.

She did. She sounded even more frazzled than before. I got the location of the facility Kyle was in. When I asked Kay when she had last visited Kyle, she responded that she had been buried at work, which I assumed meant—not recently.

When I pulled into the ramp attached to the institution, my first thought was how large the place was. I knew it was only for kids, not adults. Could there be that many kids with 'mental' health problems? When I checked in at the lobby, I was told only family could visit. When I told the receptionist that I was there on the request of Kyle's mother, the young woman responded that if Mrs. Winstad gave her permission, I would be allowed to visit. I immediately called Kay's number. Naturally it was busy. I left a message. Rather than sit in a place that depressed me, although it was new and bright, not knowing when she would have time from her busy schedule to return my call, I left.

Sure enough, she didn't call back until that evening. She said she'd call and give the facility the OK for me to see Kyle. She didn't explain or apologize for my wild goose chase. Grr… I decided to run over to Abby and Abe's to see my youngest grandchildren and relish in their happy family. In my family, family was the priority. Lou and I had always had a happy, symbiotic relationship with all our kids. My kids were each other's best friends and, as I've mentioned, the in-laws and cousins loved each other. I wondered at how people got into circumstances like Kay and Kyle's. I certainly, like anybody I suppose, didn't like to feel judgmental or inadequate, but I was feeling both. Oh well. I mentally committed to trying with Kyle.

The next morning, I called the facility, not trusting Kay, and, of course, they had not received approval from Kay. I called her and, surprisingly, she answered. It sounded like she was in a gym or workout club from the background noise I could decipher. She said she would call as soon as we hung up. Again, no apology. Not trusting her, I waited and hour and checked. Still no approval. I was beginning to understand the genesis of Kyle's afflictions.

It was very difficult not to be judgmental. I realized she was under a lot of pressure, but her priority certainly didn't seem to be her son. When I had talked to the receptionist, she had told me Kyle's last name was Morgan—not Winstad. So, something else was going on: a second marriage on the rocks for Kay? Was Kyle possibly a stepchild? Wasn't the father or maybe stepfather involved at all? Possibly not if one was overseas, but what about the other one? Well, none of this was Kyle's fault. Although feeling reticent, I resolved to try to help Kyle.

I couldn't help but think: in the orientation to the advocate program they gave us statistics about the large number of single mothers in the Black community. Here, I wasn't sure what the numbers were and Kay and Kyle's community was about as White as you could get. I'd take Wanda and Marsh's circumstances over these two, anytime.

I gave Kay an entire day and called the mental health facility the next morning. She had called, so I headed out. When I once again checked in at the reception, a different receptionist told me Kyle did not want to see me, which, I guess, didn't really surprise me. I asked if I could see a therapist or whomever was working with Kyle. After some himming and humming, she made a call and told me to take a seat. After about fifteen minutes, a young man with jeans showing under a white medical coat showed up. He said they were having very little success with Kyle. If his mother thought I could help, he was fine with it.

On the way up to the third floor, the young fellow told me that Kyle's 'escape' was internet games and that he was pretty much addicted to them. If his 'game' privileges were taken away, he pretty much clammed up. In group sessions he was unresponsive. Sounded like a catch-22. He wasn't connecting to people either way.

When I was shown into Kyle's room, which was bright and clean like the lobby, not at all physically depressing, there he was at his tablet or whatever it was, engrossed, and the same explosions I had heard before filled the room. He gave no recognition that we had entered the room. The young man raised his eyes at me and shrugged, leaving without a word.

I pulled up a chair and sat next to Kyle who was at a table— more like a desk. For a while I tried to see what the game was about, but he completely ignored me. I finally asked, again, if he could take a break from his game and we could chat. Once again, he refreshed my memory that I was not his father. I countered with I was sorry his father had had to leave for a job overseas. That his mother wanted me to visit with him. "Leave me alone," was all he said and disappeared into his game. I sat there for quite a while. It seemed like an hour but was probably half that. I, of course, hoped he would relent, but the kid at least had stamina. I left, feeling more than inadequate, figuring I'd keep coming back until somebody won the battle of attrition.

Kyle won.

I diligently had gone into see him—'seeing' is about all that happened—twice a week, same time commitment as my role as an advocate. Most days he was 'playing' a video game. Some days, I assumed as a punishment for being belligerent and non-responsive, he would have lost his 'gaming' privileges. Those days he was either watching TV or pretending to be asleep. The only time he acknowledged my presence was to remind me that I wasn't his father. Sometimes I tried creativity…dressing up in a disguise for instance. But the kid was remarkably persistent. I wondered if with that kind of tenacity, he could be successful at…something.

I totally felt like I was wasting my time and had lost any patience I had had. Whenever I'd call the director, she'd say to keep trying. When I'd call Kay, I'd rarely get ahold of her, and she rarely called back. If I did get ahold of her, I'd ask if she was able to get Kyle to talk or even respond, she'd say something like "a little." She told me a new, young intern had set up Roku or something and he was a good 'gamer' and he and Kyle were competing…playing together. That "Maybe I should have tried that." I almost told her to get…well you know. I don't think I had ever said that to anybody, but all my hours of wasted effort and this was the thanks I got? No thank you.

I had gone out for dinner or drinks with Rose and Allegra a few times throughout the Kyle ordeal. Rose, true to her word, wouldn't bring up Wanda or Marsh, and true to my word, I had promised not to badger her. Although I could tell she was conflicted with something. The three of us had so much fun going out though, she could mask it quite well. Then the last time she told me to give Lee a call. Oh, oh. If something was up with Ed, as I assumed, I wondered why Lee wouldn't have called me, herself.

I called Lee the next day but had to leave a message. A couple days went by, and she hadn't called me back. I really wanted to just stop by a Thursday gathering, but I was sure that would doom me with the smarmy director. Instead, I called Ona, who informed me that Asia had left the program, that Ed hadn't been showing up Thursdays, and that everyone was pretty sure Asia and Ed were a 'thing'! I asked if Rose or any of the group had had another 'meeting' with Wanda. She told me Rose and she had both approached Wanda, but Wanda had "demurred." She also told me Wanda had not been her gregarious self lately. Well…ya think!?

I wanted to call the director, but I didn't dare. I also didn't dare to just drop by Wanda's, which I wanted to do because I was fairly going insane. The summer was slipping by, and I was worried sick about Marsh. Was he being read to? I dreaded the thought that he'd show up for school like so many kids in his neighborhood: angry, behind developmentally, feeling like he didn't belong, potentially doomed from the get-go. I hadn't been worried about that at all until the Ed intervention. Marshawn was smart, curious and I had felt would start school ahead of most. Now I wasn't sure.

I tried Lee, again, wondering why she wasn't returning my calls. I left a message saying I apologized for bugging her, that if everything was alright with Ed and Wanda, was this also true for Marsh? That I couldn't quit worrying. I mentioned I had been told Ed was not showing up and that neither Marsh nor Wanda were their happy old selves. Was Marshawn going to be ok starting school in the next few weeks? I also mentioned I heard Asia had quit. What was up there?"

She called me back in ten minutes: "Hey, Ryan. How are you?" No exuberance, no humor in her voice. Not like Lee.

"Hi, Lee," I said. "How are things with you?"

"Oh, just grand. Sorry I didn't call you back before. I don't enjoy being stuck in the frickin' middle here!" She was obviously angry. At me?

"What…" I started.

"Look, have you become an advocate for another kid?"

Crap! "No. I mean yes. I mean I still consider myself Marshawn's advocate."

"What about this other White kid then? Ed is out of the picture. Wanda is in tough shape, of course. Marsh's being a little brat…"

"Who told you I was acting as an advocate for someone else?" I interrupted.

"Your director or whatever she is. Says you're not available no more. That she'd try to find another advocate. Maybe a Black man or woman so we don't run into the problems we did with you."

"What problems with me? The problems were with Ed. Doesn't she see this? "But—"

"No 'buts' buddy. You go take care of your rich White kid. I'm surprised at you, Ryan. You know? See ya around," and she hung up.

CHAPTER 14

Well, my ancestors' Viking genes completely ransacked the complacent ones, stomped on them, kicked them out the door. I had never been so angry. Maybe I should have waited until I cooled down; maybe not. But I immediately called the director. Of course, she didn't answer. When her voice said to leave a message, I hung up. I really was afraid of what I might say. Said "bull" to myself and called right back. I knew she had my number in her phone and so she could avoid me interminably if she wanted. I fumbled around for a while, trying to find the words, so angry I couldn't formulate a coherent sentence. Finally, I just told her I knew what she had done, and I wasn't going to stand for it. If she didn't call me back by the end of the day, I was going over her head. What would her supervisor think of her siccing me on an emotionally and mentally disturbed kid outside the program? That I should retain being Marshawn's advocate now that the replacement Ed guy was no longer in the picture. That I wasn't going to let this go. I almost said 'there!' which wouldn't have sounded as tough as I felt. So, I just hung up.

She called back later that night, at 11:30, probably expecting me to be asleep. I wasn't. She told me I had abused my advocacy role by attending that Thursday meeting, had failed as Kyle's advocate, and she would be withdrawing me from the program. I countered that I would talk with Wanda and Marsh. If they wanted me to resume my role as advocate for Marshawn, we could take it up with her supervisors. She said I wouldn't dare contact Wanda without her permission. I replied, "Watch me!" This time sounding as tough as I felt.

I didn't know what the director's problem was. Was it a control issue? This was a new program. Sometimes it takes a while to find the right people to run a program. I kinda figured she was having some trouble and was over-reacting—maybe due to a feeling of inadequacy?

I headed to bed, but my pillow felt like a hot rock. I knew my Viking genes were ready for war, not sleep. I always read a novel in bed until my eyes drooped. Didn't work this night. I'm not sure when I finally did fall asleep, but it was after I'd determined to show up the next day at the Deasel garage and hope Lee was there.

She was. I walked in to find her and Fat Albert behind a counter. She sent Albert out into the garage area, walked out from behind the counter, leaned her rear against it, crossed her arms, raised one eyebrow, and stood looking down at me. Her hair, today, was green and kind of spiky. She looked good in her greasy cut-off t-shirt and tight jeans. Intimidating but good.

It took me a while, but I calmed her down. Explained why what had happened had happened. When the time felt right, I asked if she thought Wanda would agree to sit down with me, Marshawn and, I hoped, her…to discuss the situation. She had listened, the entire time looking down at me with only one arresting but skeptical eye open.

When I asked how Wanda was handling the breakup, Lee stood up, hands on hips, looking totally like (and I can't believe I'm saying this) a sexy Amazon…I mean she was a lot of woman. She was frightening. I wasn't even sure what she might do. She hadn't said a word throughout my entire one-sided inquisition, only occasionally nodding. She walked up to me, I refused to take a step back—which is what I would have done if my irate genes were not now controlling me—and held my ground. She leaned down, cradled my head ('gently' I have to say) in her hands, and kissed my forehead. "Look, I know you're a good dude. I've always liked you. Really liked you! More importantly, Wanda and Marsh like you. But you do remember Wanda's stubbornness? Well, once she hears your handmaid's tale—the lady director must enjoy subjugating men—I think I can convince Miss Stubborn to reassess. Unless I call you, let's say this coming Monday night? At Wanda's. I suppose you want dinner?"

"Oh…" I started.

She laughed. Put her arm around my shoulder, gave me a little sideways squeeze, and headed me toward the door with a pat on the butt. "After your ordeal, you deserve a meal. If nothing else, Ed left Wanda a better cook."

"Should I pick up some…"

She opened the door, pushed me out and said, "See you Monday."

I climbed into my old Toyota and sat there, thoughts running through my mind like lemmings. I was concerned how ending with Ed would affect Wanda's confidence. How it would affect how she has men in her life. Would she trust me less?

Most prevalent now, though, was what Monday might look like. Whew!

But prevalent as well: Lee's reference to *Handmaid's Tale* and her illusion to the reverse —women subjugating men. I didn't want to think that because she was a giant Black woman in a garage that it surprised me she knew the story. I had completely, just recently of course, lost or at least *wanted* to lose, any preconceptions or 'implicit biases' I may have had regarding Black, or any other color, people who may or may not have had a 'higher' education—I really didn't know how far Lee's education had gone—but Margaret Atwood, the author of *The Handmaid's Tale,* was not an easy read. Of course, it had already been a film, an opera, as well as a television series. Regardless, you could walk down a street, heck a street on a college campus, and not one in five...even if they had heard of *The Handmaid's Tale*...could tell you what the implicit meaning of the tale was. On top of that, to use it as a reverse analogy to decipher what may very well be the director's motives, totally blew me away. I wish I could write well enough to include this in a story, just to show people not to judge. Cool. Lee was quite the...personality.

I had received a text from Lee to show up at 5:30 and to bring a bottle of wine. There was a 'no drinking' rule in the program. Wise. Even if this wasn't an 'official' advocate visit, I wasn't going to give the director any ammunition. I would just leave the wine with Wanda. It was August and was looking to be a hot August night. I usually wear tennis shoes and white athletic socks when I wear shorts, which I rarely wear as my legs are skinny and a whiter shade of pale. So, knowing that I would be ridiculed in that attire, I went out and bought a pair of Birkenstock sandals and rather than my standard golf shirt, I picked up a t-shirt that read: "The beatings will continue until morale improves." When I looked at myself in the mirror, I realized my legs didn't look so inglorious with the sandals on. I kinda liked the subtle transformation, including the snazzy, ironic t-shirt. Cool.

I arrived right at 5:30 p.m. on the dot, of course. When I pulled up in my newly purchased Honda Ridgeline—my newly arrived Viking genes having convinced me I needed new, more manly wheels—I noticed that almost everyone in the neighborhood was outside either sitting on the stoop or on lawn chairs in their yard. Although it did bug me that so many didn't bother to keep up their yards, it was really cool. Actually, it was really hot—why everyone was outside. It was a friendly atmosphere. Everybody having fun, partying. Gave me a new, more positive view of the neighborhood.

Wanda's yard was freshly mowed, and Lee and Wanda were sitting on lawn chairs, Marsh bouncing a ball off the front stoop. The screen door had been fixed a while ago, and although the house badly needed a paint job, the usual flowers made the house look homey. I got out of the car but stood there for a moment assessing how the scene might unfold. I was nervous as hell. I waved weakly but got no wave in return. Great. I hesitantly got out of the truck.

Finally, Lee, looking both frightening and fetching in rather short cut-off jean shorts and a halter, yelled, "Nice car. Get your skinny little butt over here. Quit your pathetic wimpy-ass waving." She then said something to Marsh, who had frozen, ball in hand. Suddenly he whipped the ball at me. I had grown up playing baseball, so had no problem snatching the ball out of the air with one hand.

"Oo-ee!" Lee hollered. "Did you see that, Marsh?"

I really had no idea how to act…how friendly, how reserved. What seemed natural was to walk past the two women, stop just short of Marsh, and toss him an easy underhand throw. He caught it adeptly, apparently having thrown a considerable number of balls against the stoop. "You got a glove?" I asked. He shook his head. "You know I got a glove just your size that belonged to my son, Christopher, when he was your age. You remember Chris?"

Marsh nodded, said, "He's too big to be your son."

"He wasn't always big. He used to be your size," I said, on one knee to get down to his level, though he was keeping his distance.

"Where's Sadie?" he asked.

"You want to see Sadie again?" He smiled (aha!) and nodded his head vigorously. "I think I can arrange that," I said. I turned to Wanda and asked if I could give Marsh Chris's baseball glove.

Wanda didn't answer and Lee knocked her with her elbow and told me, "Yeah. Great. Problem is, all the kids in the neighborhood want to play basketball. Marsh's legs ain't so long so he's at a disadvantage. He got nobody to play catch with."

"Well, I think I can take care of that. You got a bat?" I asked, poking him in the arm. His eyes lit up knowing what was coming. "I got a couple of those lying around. Hey, can I get a hug?" He nodded and slowly walked to me. I scooped him up, hugged him hard and said, "Have you gotten any stronger?" And he squeezed. I was afraid I was going to cry.

I set him down, held his hand and walked him over to Wanda. "Would you introduce me to this woman, please."

He giggled. "You knows who she is."

Wanda corrected him, "You *know* who she is."

I looked directly at Wanda. "And is she going to let me back into her life?"

Wanda looked down and didn't answer. Marsh said, "Mommy?" She then looked at Marsh, then Lee, then up at me and nodded. "If you stick around this time." She hadn't lost her sense of humor.

I knuckled Lee. Wanted to hug both of them. But decided to ease into my apparent redemption. I couldn't keep the thought out of my mind: What's going to come down with the director? I knew well: being in the right doesn't always work out right.

I had asked Wanda to call and speak to the director about me retaking over the role of advocate for Marsh. On Wednesday she called me and said: "Dat witch says you can't be no advocate for nobody."

I laughed. I mentioned her use of vernacular.

"Don't know no 'vernacular' wise ass," she responded. "But when some smarty White ass witch talks down to me, I forget to talk polite."

"What did you do?"

"I handed my phone to Marsh. He told her, 'I want Ryan for to be my advoke.'" She giggled conspiratorially. "Then he hung up on her."

I didn't know what to think. It was ironic that, considering the intent of the program she was supposed to operate, she'd talk 'down' to a parent in the program. But she was the director. I guess history has shown us directors, even presidents, are not always wise. It was obvious she was having difficulties. If you give small people big power, it can create an awful lot of problems. I had had some bosses who were inadequate, and their way of coping was to dictate without reason. People in over their heads needed to get out before they drown, bringing other undeserving people down with them. Like me. I'm guessing I wasn't the only person she was having trouble with. I wasn't sure why Asia quit...or could have been fired—it wouldn't, I'm sure, be unlikely if Asia and Ed had hooked up.

I was, naturally, put off by conniving, scheming, manipulative people, but here I was scheming, myself. I was not going to give up being Marsh's advocate, so 'conniving' it would have to be. First thing I did was call up Ona and a few of the parents to see if I could get any dirt on the director. Ona, of course, never had anything bad to say about anybody. But when I asked if she had had to deal with the director about Jake, her sometime boyfriend, not always being around, Ona had cleared her throat and told me, "Yes." That several times the director had said that Jake had to "shit or get off the pot," which she hadn't understood until Jake explained it to her. But the director had let it slide, she said. That she had seemed rather disorganized and had not really followed up—as Jake had still been inconsistent. Although saying he wanted to be there for Remmi, he was unreliable. I wanted to explain just how reliable a friend I could be relationship-wise but bit my tongue.

Other parents said that they hadn't had much to do with her but that they weren't exactly impressed. When I tried a few of the other advocates, Dale, the only Black advocate, didn't hold back. He was a retired coach for kids and said he definitely felt she was condescending, telling him she was concerned about him advocating for Andrea and Juan, also Black, and their son who was adopted. Dale had coached one of their friends' kids and so they had requested him. She had questioned whether he had experience with adopted kids. He said he had asked her what that had to do with the price of pickled pork feet. She had responded that since more White people adopt than Black people, maybe their advocate should be White. He had hung up on her and complained to the Minnesota Education Department, discovering his wasn't the only complaint. Several other advocates also had negative things to say.

So, aha! The conniving dark recesses of my nature suddenly lit up. I, it seemed, was not the only one suffering from the inadequacies of the director. I also wondered what her boss would think of her little blackmailing scheme with me. Was she vulnerable to a little blackmailing herself?

I decided that scheming was one thing, blackmail was another. So, I figured I'd go to the same guy at the state that Dale had. Bring Wanda and Marshawn along to help plead my case. When you launch a program, you need a top-notch person in charge to ensure success, someone who needs to be made aware, and open to consideration, if subordinates were inadequate.

It worked! I was really impressed with Wanda. She was totally confident and made me blush when she explained how good I had been for Marshawn...*and her.* The coolest though was Marsh.

When Wanda and I sat in front of this guy's big desk, Marsh crawled up into my lap. What a smart little shit. What could the guy say?

A couple days later I got a message on my phone from the director. What a...be-atch. Said she was going to watch my every step. It appeared she might seek retribution. I wondered what had happened with her at the hands of *her* superior. Something must have? I'd never met her but some of the other advocates had. They said she isn't very attractive, maybe due to her personality, but seems to think she is. She has sort of bleached-blonde hair and applies fake suntan heavy-duty. Dresses in suits, sometimes wearing a tie. Sounded weird to me. Maybe I should feel sorry for her? Nahh...she'd become an adversary. 'Watch my every step!?' Screw her. I needed to stand up to her. I think I wanted to make Lee proud.

When the next Monday came around, I showed up early with a new book as well as a baseball glove and bat I had had laying around. Wanda sat on the front stoop in a Twins t-shirt (good—funny), shorts, knee-high socks, tennies, and a baseball cap. Marsh and I squared up right off, facing each other, he now with a glove, me assuming I didn't need one. It took a while to get him used to the baseball mitt. It was a little big for him and he got frustrated. Said he'd rather catch it barehanded.

"But if I throw the ball overhand, which is harder," I explained, "it will hurt if you don't catch it with your glove. You see players on TV catching without a glove?"

He frowned. "Show me," he yelled.

I threw it as soft as I could overhand. Although he had the glove on, he tried to catch it barehanded with his right hand. He tried not to show it, but when it bounced off his hand it stung. He picked up the ball, looked at me, and almost took my head off. Man did the kid have an arm. I ducked and tried to catch it with my bare hands, but no way—it stung me like crazy as it ricocheted off.

Wanda thought this was quite hilarious. She yelled, laughing: *You* need a glove, Ryan."

"Yeah, you need a glove, Rine," Marsh quipped, his fat cheeks bulging in a huge smile.

I picked up the ball. "Ok, I'll toss it underhand, but just try to catch it with your mitt. OK?"

This time he caught it by cradling it against his chest, and I suppose like he had seen on TV, he turned his left shoulder toward me and whipped the ball to me like a shortstop who has just fielded a grounder and was throwing to first.

Well, being about just five feet away, I just had time to duck out of the way. No chance to try to catch it. And it thudded into the side of my brand-new shiny white Honda Ridgeline. Sure enough, when I retrieved the ball, there was a brand-new shiny dent in the rider's door. Wanda, of course, was laughing hysterically on the stoop. So was Marsh, who thought this was quite hilarious as well. The kid had an arm.

"Ok. I'll bring my mitt next time," I said. "Since you don't have anyone to play catch with in the neighborhood, let me show you something." I stood next to him and threw the ball straight up and caught it. Did this several times. "Now you throw it up and catch it yourself, in your glove."

I handed him the ball, and when he threw it, he tried to draw rain and it ended up in the neighbor's yard. They were all drinking beer, sitting in lawn (even though there wasn't one) chairs.

They threw the ball back yelling, "Whooey! Kid's got an arm."

I waved. "Alright," I explained to the kid. "Don't try to throw it so high. Just try to get it straight up, and when it comes down, catch it in the web of your glove." I cushioned the ball in the web to show him. "Now, here. Straight up."

It was a little better, and he ran after it with his arm extended straight out, having no chance to catch it.

"Ok, I'll throw it up, you catch it. But don't stick your arm straight out. You'll never catch it that way."

"But I don't want it to hit me," he whined.

"The farther your hand is away from your eyes," I patiently explained, "the more likely it is to hit you."

Marsh looked at me skeptically. I held his glove right next to his ear. "Catch it here and lock it into your glove." More skepticism. "Ready?" I asked. A slight nod.

I made a big full body motion of tossing it up so he could follow it. And he did. He held his glove right next to his ear and watched the ball as it plopped him squarely between the eyes. He didn't react immediately, almost as if the ball had not just bounced off his face. He slowly removed the glove and threw it at me.

Wanda's head was between her knees, her body shaking. "Not funny!" Marsh yelled. Then he eyed the bat laying in the grass. I was pretty sure he thought of it more as a weapon.

"I want to bat," he said, I felt, rather malevolently.

I borrowed Wanda's baseball cap and set it down for home plate. Showed him how to hold the bat and had him take a couple practice swings. He caught on right away. I backed off a bit and bent to send him an easy underhand pitch. I didn't like the look in his eye.

He swung the bat ferociously, missing the first few by a mile. I didn't know if he was aiming for the 'fence'…or me. Out of self-preservation, I called time out and showed him how to choke-up on the bat. "Now, just try to tap the ball back to me, keeping your eye on the ball."

When he heard the word 'eye' he got that skeptical look on his face again. But I backed up just a bit farther and tossed him a slow, underhand strike. He still swung for the fence—or me—and the knob on the handle whopped him in the side.

I couldn't tell if he was going to cry or was just getting more determined. I took the bat and demonstrated how to just sort of tap-bunt it. Not a full swing. "See?" I asked.

He took the bat back and did what I showed him, and he hit the ball almost every time. He went about it methodically, like he had a plan.

"Ok, lemme just hit it," he eventually said, and lost the choke-up.

I'm telling you the truth. I backed off aways and got ready to toss him the ball. Well, my little exercise had worked. He kept his eye on the ball, swung for the fence, and the ball skinned my ear—woulda torn my earring right off, if I had had one. (All the Deasels had them and I had thought, why not the new me?) Then I heard the crash. When I turned, a gaping eye just the size of a baseball stared at me from the rider's side window. Didn't know a ball could do that.

Although Wanda had by now stopped laughing and had her hand over her mouth, Marsh smiled, no apology, flipped the bat like he'd hit a homerun, and walked "home" you might say—into the house. I knew the little shit had had a plan. Son-of-a-gun. Definitely a smart little runt. Of course, there's my now not-so-new Ridgeline.

The book I had brought was *Where the Sidewalk Ends* by Shel Silverstein. So, the three of us settled on the couch, a smug Marsh climbed right up into my lap. He cracked up immediately when he saw the cover. If you've never seen it, it's a comical sketch of a sideways view of a sidewalk suspended in space. A dog's hind legs and tail dangling through a hole in the sidewalk and two kids peeking over the edge.

He quickly turned the page to another sketch, and I read Shel's intro aloud: "There is a place where the sidewalk ends. And before the street begins. And there the grass grows soft and white. And there the sun burns crimson bright. And there the moon-bird rests from his flight. To cool in the peppermint wind. Let us leave this place where the smoke blows black."

He giggled and touched with his fingers the humorous sketch. But when I read the poems, although fantastical, he was serious as a monk. In Silverstein's remarkable imagination, a boy turns into a television set, a girl eats a whale, Sara Cynthia Stout will not take the garbage out, shoes fly, and crocodiles go to the dentist. He particularly liked the idea of washing his shadow. He smoothed his fingers over the poem for several minutes, deep in thought. Then, finally, he started to laugh.

So, Shel was a hit, the visit was a success. Wanda, not sharing in Marsh's mirth, had been eerily quiet.

When I picked them up on Thursday…me driving once again in Wanda's car with Marsh buckled in the back. The Ridgeline parked out front. "Where's the hole?" he asked as soon as we took off.

"Gone," I answered. (Figured I'd get a little revenge.)

"Where'd it go?"

"I have it on a shelf in my garage," I responded—my attempt at being Shel, I suppose. I had always tried to spoof my kids to get them thinking. Shel had been a favorite of theirs. They had liked all his books.

Marsh sat there considering my response.

"I want to see it," he finally said.

"You can't see a hole," I said and looked at his very serious face in the rearview mirror.

"Uh-uh," he finally said.

"Uh-uh what?"

"You can't put no hole on a shelf," he said, not sounding totally sure of himself.

"Well, it's not in the window anymore. Where'd it go?"

"Ma, where'd it go?"

Wanda had been smiling the whole time. She corrected his misuse of "no hole" and said: "Why don't you ask Ryan to bring it over and put it back in the window?" Wise-ass kids have wise-ass mothers.

"Yeah!" he spouted. "I want it back in the window where it belongs."

Smart mom; smart kid.

At our meeting, I discovered that Arnie, Jay White Cloud's kid, liked basketball the best. Of course, at four years of age he was almost as tall as Wanda, so no wonder. But Jay said they play catch a lot, too…with both a baseball and a football. Ooh, football, cool. I had a feeling Marsh would like football. I'd wait till fall. Get him a football. Jay said that he'd gone in with some of his neighbors and they had put up a backboard on one of the decent driveways. I asked if Monday I could bring Marsh over. Jay had looked at me in his quiet way and said, "You better ask Marshawn about that."

I wasn't going to ask Marsh. It seemed clear to me we had to go, but I remembered that at the last ill-advised and probably ill-fated meeting, Marsh and Arnie had not talked. "Can we come over? I'll bring our baseball gloves." I guessed this was a 'neighborhood' issue, and so a racial thing as well. A weird one: the Indians vs. the Blacks. I felt like it was my job to fix this for Marsh and Arnie.

"Sure," Jay answered.

"Around six?"

"Sure," Jay answered.

On the way home I mentioned to Marsh that Arnie played catch with his dad and liked basketball.

"I'm too short for basketball," he had replied.

"How about Monday we have a little outing?" I suggested.

"Yeah. Can we get ice cream? Or pizza?"

I looked over at Wanda, who was looking at me with her eye raised. "Maybe," I said and smiled. "It's up to your mother."

When I came over Monday, Marsh came running out the front door. "Where's dat hole?" he hollered, pointing at the window.

Took me by surprise, one of the many times to come where I'd think he'd forgotten about something. "I lost it," I came up with.

He stopped and looked at me for a while. "Lost it where?"

"I have no idea," I said.

Another pause, thinking. "Well, you gotta find it."

"'Have to find it,'" from Wanda, now on the stoop.

"How?" I asked. "I can't see it."

Stumped, he put his hands on his hips as I'd seen his mother do a million times.

"I brought my glove," and I held it up. "Go get yours. He gave me one last dirty look, turned and ran past Wanda into the house.

"You sure this is a good idea going over to the White Clouds?" she asked as she walked down the steps.

I had called her and told her my idea. "Why not?" I answered. "You don't want Marsh to be friends with Arnie because he's an Indian?"

Her eyes flashed. "That's not it, as you know, wiseass. What about Latrell and the neighborhood kids? What are they gunna—"

And Marsh burst out the door and down the steps. Put his glove on and pretended to throw—I suppose a ball—at my car. "Well, go get it," he said.

"Go get what?"

"The ball. It's in the car."

"Oh? And how'd it get in the car?"

"It went through the hole," he said like I was stupid.

"What hole?" I asked, smiling.

"The one in the window. You just can't see it."

Well, Wanda and I had a good laugh at the smart little wiseass. Marsh and I played catch for a while. I convinced him he didn't have to try to take my head off every time he threw me the ball. He had obviously been practicing catching the ball. He still missed most but tried hard and caught quite a few.

When we climbed in the car with our mitts, Marsh asked if we were getting pizza. I told him yes, but we were stopping somewhere else first. When we pulled up to Jay's, Marsh unhooked his seat belt and sat up. "This is Arnie's!" he said, alarmed.

"Yup," I said, like it was nothing out of the ordinary.

Marsh sat back in his seat. "Arnie's mad at me," he said.

"Grab your mitt and we'll check it out."

"He ain't gonna like dat" he said.

"He isn't going to like *that*," Wanda corrected.

"Right," Marsh said. "Zackly."

I couldn't help but laugh again. "C'mon. Grab your mitt." And we walked to the front porch.

Jay walked out of his house with Arnie trailing behind. The house had been white at one time, but little paint remained. There was no grass or flowers like at Wanda's. Old tricycles and other toys were scattered around the yard. Everything randomly left where it appeared it had fallen out of the sky. I noticed hanging on the covered front porch was the front bench seat from some old car or truck. It was suspended from the porch's overhang.

My first thought was *What a mess*. And, *Really, an old car or truck seat for a porch swing?*

"Want a beer or something?" Jay asked. Wanda said sure. I had to decline. Jay came back with a beer and two large glasses of water.

"You're not having one, Jay?" I asked, as we walked up onto a rather rickety porch.

"Nah. Don't drink."

I glanced at the 'swing.' Have a seat, Jay said. "It's comfortable."

I was surprised. It was old enough to have springs and was indeed comfortable.

"It's from my old pickup out back," Jay explained. "The truck's pretty much just a skeleton, now. It's pretty much stripped of parts, except for the bed and rear tires."

I frowned. "Why only rear tires?"

"Well, I used all the engine parts, front tires, and other stuff. Now it'll be a trailer, so need the wheels. Not sure what to do with the cab. I'll think of something."

I kicked myself. I didn't think I was judgmental, but here I was again. Implicit bias I guess you'd say. I'm guessing Jay didn't think the yard was messy. Who cared what the house looked like? It sheltered him and Arnie. It served its function. As I pushed against the covered porch floor, I started to swing in the most comfortable swing I'd ever sat on. How cool. Why throw it away? Create waste? Jay and his culture were the real recyclers.

We had a game of catch between the four of us. Arnie, being more physically mature, was catching better than Marsh. I saw that bothered Marsh. I knew he'd be practicing more. We even tossed a football around a bit. Marsh looked like a natural.

On the way to get pizza, Marsh asked Wanda not to tell Latrell about playing with Arnie. I pointed out that school was starting in a few weeks. Were his only friends at school going to be Latrell and his buddies?

He hadn't answered.

"Don't you want to be friends with Arnie? How about Remmi? So, if Latrell didn't want you to be friends with Remmi, you wouldn't?"

Still no answer.

I asked what if Sadie, Abby and Abe's three-year-old who he had rescued in the bouncy thing, was in his class. Wouldn't he want to be friends with her?

At the sound of Sadie's name, Marsh lit up. "Sadie!" he yelled. "Can we see Sadie?"

I smiled in the rearview mirror. "It's her birthday next week. Wanna go to the party?"

Wanda looked over at me, smiled, whispered, "Nice job." She turned, looked at Marsh who was jumping up and down as best he could restrained by his seat belt. "Of course. We'll need to find a present."

"Yeah, yea!"

We decided to invite the Deasels as well. Most came. Abby and Abe's house was too small for all of us and the Deasels, but fortunately it was a nice August day, sunny and not too warm. Perfect for a barbecue. They lived on a hill with about a three-acre yard, so Marsh and my grands had plenty of room to roam. None of the Deasels were married or had any kids. Lee was the only one with a significant other, and she and Colleen both showed up. Colleen played with the kids the most. I wondered if adoption was in the future. I wondered why the Deasel giants had no wives or, apparently, even girlfriends, but felt that was none of my business. They'd tell me if they wanted. But with no cousins of his own, it seemed like my grands had adopted Marsh. Wanda mixed well, which really made me happy and...proud, I guess. My family thought she was a stitch. I probably ended up talking to Lee more than anyone. Got a stiff neck. She was, fortunately, supportive of me being back in the picture. It was a great day. Everybody got along!

I had asked my daughter, Abby, if she would be concerned what the neighbors in this very white neighborhood might think about Black giants visiting. "I don't care," she had answered. "Screw em if it bothers them."

Sunday of the week before school started, I got a tweet from the director. She said that the aid at the mental health facility that had 'gamed' with Kyle had left and Kyle had withdrawn again. She said he may not be able to return to school. "Nice job you did there," she told me, flaring my guilt and pissing me off.

I shot back a message that Marsh was doing great, would be well-prepared for kindergarten, and we had gotten mostly over his dilemma with the neighborhood kids. Because Marsh would be good friends with Arnie, a Native American, and Remmi, a Bahamian, as well as the diverse range of kids in the daycare group, maybe things would be cool in school. Maybe he was going to be a leader. If he was a good example, maybe everyone gets along. Wasn't that the idea of the program? Everyone getting along? More worthwhile from my perspective than dealing with a screwed up, spoiled, rich White kid who couldn't be helped even by mental health professionals? It wasn't that I didn't wish him well. But I didn't think I could've helped him.

I didn't get a response from her. This worried me.

Had I said all that hoping it would alleviate some of my guilt? I really didn't feel it was my fault I had felt no connection at all to Kyle. He made it clear he wanted no connection with me. I did try. Oddly, Kyle's affliction—a White kid's affliction, or rich kid's, or whatever you'd call it—turned out *not* to be in my wheelhouse. But Wanda and Marsh were. I flashed back to that first night. Man, I was happy I had become an advocate. It had opened up a new world for me...literally and figuratively. My world was much larger...and more interesting.

CHAPTER 15

That Monday I decided to have Marsh, Wanda, and I take turns reading from *Where the Sidewalk Ends*. With Marsh in my lap, I whispered each word in his ear and helped him with the pronunciation of tough words. He did pretty good with most of it. I felt like he was almost reading, even if he was really just beginning to memorize the words, which was cool, too, of course. What was really cool, I thought, was even while he struggled a bit when we reread, he still was able to focus on and 'got' Shel's humor and now would laugh like a crazy man, leaving Wanda and I pretty much hysterical. Wanda was even better than me at reading the poems funny. Marsh laughed the hardest at his mother.

Things, remarkably, had been rolling along smoothy. All, thank God, seemed good. September, and school was right around the corner. Every time I thought about this, I got butterflies. For the final Thursday meeting before school was to start, each child going to kindergarten was supposed to tell us their favorite book and read or recite from memory a short selection from it to the group. Marsh picked the title poem "Where the Sidewalk Ends" to read, which I thought was weird because it was one of the only ones that wasn't funny. Could he pull it off? Would he have it memorized? I knew Wanda had been working with him. I was prepared to help him if he had trouble.

At the meeting I was happy to see Marsh head right for Arnie. After a little mixing, we all sat at tables circling the room, each child with his or her parent or parents and advocate for the readings. I was really impressed. The kids did well, all with minimal prompting. When it got to Marsh, who was last, he held up the book, showing the cover, and looked around the room and waited so long, we all, me especially, started to get nervous. I was just about to do a little prompting, myself, when Wanda stopped me. Marsh, looking so serious, started slowly, still holding up the book, looking out at everybody, and confidently picked up momentum. The kid had memorized the verse! I looked at Wanda and choked up. He got all the words right, and more. When he was done, everyone was silent for a moment.

The verse goes:

> Yes we'll walk a walk that is measured and slow,
> And we'll go where the chalk-white arrows go.
> For the children, they mark and the children they know
> The place where the sidewalk ends.

Ok, I hadn't realized it until this time and context: this was the perfect analogy for the group heading off to school. Yup, the sidewalk now ends. The road is ahead. School starts for many. What's down there over the edge of that sidewalk? A bigger world. How would they do? Were they ready? Would they feel like they belong? I took pause. It was like I just realized how much this meant to me. Not only for Marsh, but how would Arnie fit in? Gentle Remmi? I looked around the room, caught Ona's eye. Felt Wanda's hand on my shoulder. I could see all the adults and the other advocates were thinking what I was thinking. They clearly recognized the significance of the metaphor…but the kids? I mean everybody paused. Not a sound. Can't be—right? Kids are dumb. But it was like a record stuck or a CD skipped in my mind. Like a moment lost in time. Why did Marsh pick out the only poem that wasn't funny? He couldn't have done it on purpose. Nahh!

Finally, someone clapped, almost hesitatingly. Then gradually everyone, even the dumb kids, followed suit and the clapping grew into an applause, a crescendo. Everyone was clapping for everyone. But no one was smiling or cheering. I had to look down. I was barely holding back the tears. Wanda's hand found mine.

The following Tuesday school would start. The time was here, now. It had been quite the journey. A pilgrimage. I couldn't help but feel a little—well, a lot—of dread, and a lot of excitement.

Both of which, it would turn out, were warranted.

Was this the end of the sidewalk for me, as well? Marsh was hopefully ready. Would he still need me? Would Wanda? What about Ona? Gone from my life? Even harder to consider was Lee. I'd never met a woman like her before. I couldn't imagine her out of my life, much less Wanda and Marsh. This was a new world for me, and I was now ingrained in it. My life was larger.

But Marsh…school would be no smooth sidewalk. Could Wanda be there all the time to catch him when he trips? Would I even be there to know?

EPILOGUE

How will Marsh handle grade school, his relationship with Latree and his neighborhood friends, Arnie and his Native American neighborhood buddies? Will he remain friends with Remmi who may be labeled an immigrant, a Muslim?

What will happen with Wanda's next boyfriend? How might this affect Ryan and his advocacy with Marsh? Will Marsh and Wanda stay close with Ryan's family? Will Ryan remain friends, or more, with Lee? The Deasels? Ona? Will Rose remain close with Wanda?

Find out in *The Advocate, Part II.*

ACKNOWLEDGEMENTS

J eff Mork (teacher emeritus) for pre-reading. Kathy Strunk Haeg for pre-reading and editing. Randall Hanson, inner-city youth worker, for pre-reading and insights.